Ignite

Holly S. Roberts

FOURCARATPRESS.COM

Ignite

Holly S. Roberts

Published by Four Carat Press
Copyright 2016 Holly S. Roberts
Printing History
eBook edition 2016
Paperback edition 2017

Edited by Michelle Kowalski
Cover by Fantasia Frog Designs

Chapter One

Rack

The knife wound runs down my side from under my arm to the top of my hip. It burns like a motherfucker, and the tequila does little to stop the pain as the needle sinks into my flesh. The stitches are far from professional, but they'll do the job and close the skin, keeping muscle and tissue on the inside where they belong.

Never strangle a man with a knife in his hand is my new motto. He sliced into my side before I could stop him. He's dead now and I'm alive, so I'll take it as a lesson learned. Putting up with Gomez's shit for my stupidity isn't helping me feel the love as he stitches me up.

"Fuck," he swears as he wipes his bloody hands on a blood-covered cloth. I look down at myself as he readjusts his grip on the large needle. "You can't do things halfway, can you?" he taunts as the needle punctures my skin again.

I take another pull from the bottle and suck in a breath as he works the needle through the skin on the other side and ties off another stitch. "The son of a bitch is dead, so why the hell are you complaining?" I hiss the last of the statement.

Gomez is a cold motherfucker—someone you don't cross and also someone I trust with my life. His steely dark eyes drill into mine. "Every time you pull this shit you're on light duty at the main house. I need you at full capacity. Just call me an unfeeling son of a bitch if it makes you feel better."

I laugh even though it hurts. "I've always performed my job and you know it. I'll handle whatever comes our way or die trying."

Gomez shakes his head and I see something rare in his gaze. Celina, his girlfriend, has changed him. Not in a way that will get him killed; no, it's something inside him that wasn't there before she came into his life. He's at peace with who he is and what we do. A peace that I can't manage. Will most likely never manage.

Gomez brings me out of the alcohol fog. "At least tell me you acquired more names for us?"

By "us" he means Moon's organization. Moon controls the criminal underworld of Arizona and New Mexico. Gomez is Moon's right hand. If there's a left hand, it's me. This is because Moon and Gomez understand vengeance. I won't rest until each man responsible for killing my brother Andrew is dead. Moon and Gomez want more than those last two names. They want to take down the Ocana Cartel. I'm good with that even though taking out one cartel means two more will replace it.

Moon mostly leaves the cartels alone if they remain on their side of the border and keep their drug business in Mexico. Doesn't matter that the U.S. contains the majority of their customers; Moon controls the southwest border. This is his territory and he has strict rules, which the cartels heed or die. Ocana is not playing nice and never has. We're putting an end to their border jumping.

"I have a name," I say with a painful gasp. "It will help Moon with Ocana more than it helps me find the last two responsible for my brother. I'm getting closer, though."

Gomez nods and I inhale deeply when he helps me sit up. I lift my arms and allow him to wrap gauze around my chest. The room spins and my stomach lurches. "You gonna make it?" he asks.

"Yeah, I'll fucking make it."

He grunts, which is his idea of a challenge.

I slide my legs off the dirty counter where I've been laying. We're in one of Moon's safe houses. It's a small shack that secretes mold from the walls, has minimal furniture, and windows so dirty they're nearly impossible to see through.

The sudden sting of a needle going in my arm is nothing compared to the burn in my side. What the house lacks in cleanliness it makes up for in first aid supplies, which stay hidden behind a cabinet in the bathroom. Gomez just shot me full of antibiotics. I turned down pain medication and chose the tequila, which I have more practice in handling. Pain meds mess with my head. Give me alcohol any day.

Gomez is back to assessing me. "We need to get out of here."

I'm holding onto the counter and loosen my grip to take a wobbly step forward. I *can* handle the tequila; it's the blood loss kicking my ass right now. I slap Gomez's arm away like a bird flappin' its wings. Gomez grins.

"Let's get the fuck back to the U.S.," I say with far more grit than I feel. He hands me a shirt and I shrug it on casually as if my side isn't a fireball. I do this to convince myself I can make it out of here. Pain is good. It reminds me I'm alive.

We walk between shanty houses along narrow dirt roads for an hour. We see more roaches the size of rats than we do people. This part of Tijuana is far from inviting at three in the morning. Most of the so-called homes are little more than scrap wood covered by tarps and cloth. An entire family can live in an eight by eight home. People from the U.S. don't understand poverty unless they've been to a place like this. We continue our trudge through open sewage. Breathing heavily through my mouth does little to keep the smell at bay. My head stays up and I do everything I can to look tough instead of how I feel—like bird shit dropping on my shoulder could take me down.

"Rendezvous up ahead." Gomez's hushed voice barely penetrates the fog that is now my brain. He's not dumb and knows I'm barely staying upright. His words give me the added incentive to keep my legs moving. A minute later, his hand on my arm stops me mid-step and he guides me farther into the shadows. Gomez squeezes my arm twice. He's checking out the car ahead without me. Usually it's the other way around, but I know when I need to hang back.

He releases me and maneuvers silently until I can't see him. I recognize his whistle a minute later and know all's clear. I move forward at least ten feet before I drop to my knees and then face-plant onto the ground. The world thankfully goes dark.

* * * *

I groan as I come to in the back seat of a car. I have no idea how long I've been out.

Gomez, who's sitting up front, answers the question without waiting for me to ask it aloud. "Ten minutes." He leans between the seats and hands me a bottle of water.

Austin is driving. I have no idea if Austin is his first name or last. He's Victor Corbin's enforcer. This makes him a scary dude. Austin's about 2 inches shorter than me and Gomez and he doesn't carry as much muscle. His pale blue eyes are as cold as Gomez's dark ones. Austin is a killer and one I never want to go up against. Corbin, his boss, runs the drugs and guns in Cali. We pre-arranged this pickup with Corbin. It surprises me he sent Austin. Things must be slower in California than they are in Arizona and New Mexico.

After drinking half the water, I close my eyes as the old rattle-trap car bumps along over what must be a dirt road. The last thing you want to do if you're interested in avoiding attention in Tijuana is drive something expensive. I have no doubt the engine of the car far outshines the exterior. Gomez and Austin allow me to regroup my strength while we travel.

We hit a short line of cars at the border crossing, and when it's our turn a K-9 circles the car with his handler. We aren't carrying anything that will get us in trouble, though we must appear highly suspicious. Thankfully we're on our way in a matter of minutes. The next stop we make is a private airfield, where a plane and pilot are waiting. I breathe easier once we're in the air and headed back to Arizona.

I'm seriously getting too old for this shit and I'm only thirty-three.

Chapter Two

From: Nick.Hoffman@us.gov.org
To: Beth.Hoffman@mymail.com
Dear Baby Sister,
Yeah, I know you hate when I call you that. Too bad, you will always be the baby. Life is good but dirty as in dirt everywhere. You don't need to hear all the dirty details but this man's balls are gritty and I'll leave it at that. This pretty much explains Afghanistan to a T. My friend Rack saves my sanity. This is his third tour and he knows his shit. You would like him and I know he would like you. Hint, hint!
Your favorite and only big brother,
Nick

* * * *

Beth

The men watch me around the clock. Getting my hands on a cell phone is a fluke and I still can't believe my luck. I need to send a text and get out of Peter's room quickly.

I don't have much time to think about what I send, but I need to be smart. I can delete the history after sending the text. This opens up a new set of problems. If Peter notices his missing messages, he'll check his phone account online and trace the text. If that happens, it won't be just me in danger. Fear travels through my veins and makes my already rapid heartbeat speed up even more. I put myself into this mess and now I'm endangering someone else. I shake off the fear and look back down where my fingers clench the phone.

Shakily, I type *his* number followed by my message.

This is Beth Hoffman, Nick's sister.
I'm in trouble and being held by Angelo Gimonde
Westly Ranch
Camp Springs, Montana
Phone compromised

I take a deep breath and click Send. The trembling in my fingers doubles as I delete the text history. I'm so screwed. It's little comfort that Angelo won't immediately kill me. He'll hunt Rack down and kill him first. I've endangered Rack even if he checks Angelo's name on the Internet and decides I'm not worth saving. If only I were more intelligent in the beginning and never stepped into this mess.

I don't know Rack well. He was my brother's best friend in the military. Seeing Rack through Nick's eyes really doesn't count. Nick told me more than once if I ever needed help and he wasn't around, to call Rack. A shiver passes through me. Did Nick somehow know that he wouldn't be around, that an IED would take him out only a few months before his return to the States?

I only met Rack once. It was a few months before my first wedding date. My fiancé delayed the first one and then the second. I squelch the stupidity I feel that there was ever more than one. The last few years of my life are one bad decision after another. When Rack visited me his expression had none of the carefree qualities my brother described. Oh, I expected the dangerous undertone, just not the dead eyes. His gaze held a complete lack of humanity. And still, my body betrayed me. Rack is a force of nature and like nature, he's raw and compelling. His insanely green eyes turned my insides to jelly. His muscles stretched his polo shirt to near bursting. His square jaw spoke of strength and determination. His dark hair with its closely cropped military cut took the danger he radiated up a notch. Everything about him made me think of silk sheets and hot sex. I swear, by the way his luscious mouth smirked he was reading my body like a map. He didn't miss the shortness of breath, sweaty palms, or my accelerated heartbeat. He couldn't have. God, I actually wondered if he could smell the desire my body exuded via wet panties. His eyes literally changed color to a deeper green and his nostrils flared as I came undone at his proximity. The experience was mortifying and made worse by my engagement to another man.

I held so much guilt over that one meeting. Or at least I did until I discovered my fiancé in bed with my best friend the night before our third calendar wedding date. Now my ex-best friend and ex-fiancé. I hope the two of them spend eternity together making each other miserable.

I sigh into the quiet room. Even with all the trouble I've brought down on my head, I'm a vindictive bitch and I'm not ready to forgive and forget. I check the time on the phone. Angelo will return shortly and I need to get out of Peter's room.

If Angelo finds out about the phone, he'll kill Peter for this. Peter is a young fool. He's infatuated with Angelo's lifestyle. The lifestyle of a mobster where kidnapping is just another walk in the park. I have absolutely no reason to feel sorry for Peter. Like me, he'll need to live with his decisions.

I rest the cell phone back on the nightstand and walk to the door. There are cameras in the hallway. I'm carrying one of Peter's long-sleeved flannel shirts, which is the reason I entered his room to begin with. I need Peter to pocket his phone when he returns and keep his mouth shut about leaving it behind this morning. My only chance is that Peter knows Angelo will kill him for the mistake. I still can't believe my luck in discovering it.

I pull the heavy shirt over my shoulders and head downstairs. Because of the building weather front moving in, there's a chilly wind blowing. Angelo didn't provide me with a jacket because it's the middle of summer and up until today it's been warm. That's Montana for you—one day it's in the nineties and the next in the forties. I need to exercise to drive the crazies away. It's one of the few perks I'm granted. I'm required to sit at the dinner table with Angelo each evening if he's here on the ranch. I don't consider joining him a perk, it's more a punishment. The look in Angelo's eyes is scary and predatory when he sits across from me. I'm his possession.

I met Angelo a month after my breakup with Kevin. I was not in a good place mentally and Angelo swooped in and picked up the pieces of my broken heart. I had no idea who he was. Handsome and charming, I fell for his baited hook having no idea he was the embodiment of pure evil. I shudder at the memories I've tried hard to forget even though forgetting will never happen. To make a point about those who betray him, Angelo shot one of his men in front of me and laughed when the blood splattered my face. I hyperventilated and vomited. Angelo walked from the small room with a look of disgust and locked me inside with the body for hours. Before the man died at my feet, he offered to help me escape if I slept with him. Sadly, I was willing to do anything and that included allowing Angelo's man to touch my body. He died before I agreed. That was six months ago. Sending the text is the first time I've tried to escape since.

I pull the large shirt tightly around me and head out the back door off the kitchen. I keep to a well-established path within the sphere of the outside cameras. I've learned not to incur Angelo's wrath. The consequences of no more walks aren't worth it. I'm barely holding onto my sanity as it is.

I do my best to take deep breaths and slow my breathing, allowing nature to soothe me. I struggle with the slight hill and my breath comes in small gasps. I circle the entire house. Before I can take a third trip, I notice Angelo's black pickup truck driving up the long drive.

I place my hand on my large belly.

He may be your father but I swear I'll never allow him to infect you with his evil.

Chapter Three

Rack

After Dr. Santos examined me and shot me full of more antibiotics, he shook his head while rewrapping my chest and told me to rest for the next few days. He was well aware that would never happen. I slept around the clock. One day of sleep and I craved the gym, tender wound be damned.

The stitches pull during my workout, so I take it easy—two miles on the treadmill, push-ups, chin-ups, sit-ups. Gomez attended a meeting with Moon this morning and I have the gym to myself. I'm finishing my workout and thinking about a hot shower when Celina walks in. I rise from the floor after my last ten push-ups and try to grab my shirt before she sees the blood seeping through the gauze.

Her hands go to her small waist. "Don't bother. Carlo told me what happened."

Carlo is Dr. Santos. "Whatever happened to doctor-patient confidentiality?" I grumble.

She ignores my question. "He told me to keep an eye on you and make sure you take it easy. I've already failed and you should be ashamed."

I pull the shirt over my sweaty torso. "I take it you don't want to spar this morning?"

"You're incorrigible," she returns while fighting a smile. The edges of her lips pull up before she remembers to act stern. "I'll pass until you're back to your old puny self and can put up a decent fight."

I grin and wink. "I like a challenge. You're getting better, but I can still kick your ass with one hand tied behind my back."

"One hand tied behind your back? Deal. We'll try that when you return to full strength."

I can only shake my head. She's like a Chihuahua thinking it's a Pitbull with jaws locked on a hambone. Gomez won't spar with her because he doesn't want to hurt her. I don't enjoy hurting her either, but if you live in our world, you need to accept pain and work through it. She improves each week and refuses to give up. She's gained my respect.

Loud girly music fills the room and Celina hits the treadmill. I head to my bedroom for a shower. Yeah, Santos told me to keep the stitches dry. Doesn't matter, I need a shower; I do the best I can to keep the spray directly off the wound. I smear on the foul-smelling goo Santos gave me and wrap more dressing around my chest after I'm out of the shower. Just as I'm pulling a clean T-shirt over my head, a text comes through on my cell.

I stride over and peer down at the message alert. Not a number I recognize. Picking up the phone, I enter my access code and read the text.

"Fuck," I whisper into the quiet room. "Double fuck," I swear louder.

It's Beth, Nick's sister. She's in trouble. I know exactly who Angelo Gimonde is. How Beth got mixed up with him is beyond me. I enter Westly Ranch, Camp Springs, Montana into my cell phone's browser. It pops up and gives me an address. I'm more than twenty hours away by car, which sucks because I don't know if she has twenty hours.

Angelo Gimonde's father is the head of Chicago's largest crime syndicate. Angelo killed the daughter of another mob boss a little over a year ago and then disappeared. I'd hoped their rival organization, the Laterza family, had taken him out. Hiding in bum fuck Montana is most likely the only thing that kept him alive.

When I returned stateside after Nick's death, I went to Montana and checked up on Beth. It was the coldest place on earth as far as I was concerned. Living in Phoenix makes any temperature below sixty an extreme. Beth was devastated over the loss of her brother, but she was planning her wedding and starting a new chapter in her life.

Her strength didn't surprise me. Nick was the strongest son of a bitch I ever met and he saved my life more than once. I promised to look after his baby sister if anything happened to him.

Nick was there when I got news that my brother Andrew died. I could have taken the first plane home, but instead I went out with my squad and we encountered enemy fighters. Nick took a bullet to the leg, which he could have survived. He grabbed my hand before medics took him away. "Don't forget your promise to look after Beth," he said.

"Yeah, yeah, you pussy, it's nothing but a scratch and you'll be back kicking ass in a few days," I told him. Minutes later, an IED struck the med transport and Nick died instantly.

I stayed in Afghanistan and took my rage out on insurgents before I went home. I missed my brother's funeral and Nick's. It was better that way. In the weeks after their deaths I wasn't fit for anything but killing.

Visiting Nick's sister was hard and made harder by the fact she didn't hold me responsible for his death. Didn't change the fact that I was responsible. I was there and should have taken the bullet that put Nick on the transport. It's as simple as that.

I didn't care for Beth's fiancé, but she loved him and that's all that mattered. So how the hell is she involved with Angelo Gimonde?

I pack a small bag with a few changes of clothes and write a note to Gomez. I drop it off in the security room, where I fill a larger bag with firepower.

"You want me to give this to Gomez when he returns?" Cal asks while he watches me fill the munitions bag with a little of everything.

"That's exactly what I want. He'll understand after he reads it." Gomez will understand immediately. Moon and his organization cannot be involved in what I'm about to do. There's no love lost between Moon, the Gimonde family, and the Laterza family. The problem: as big as Moon's organization is now he's still not in the same league as East Coast mafia. Moon's smart enough to know that and so is Gomez. I need to do this alone and get Beth the hell out of Angelo's hands before he strangles her like he did the last woman.

An airplane is out of the mix without Moon's authorization. I'm taking my personal Jeep and praying Moon isn't linked to what I'm about to do. Killing Angelo will bring the heat down on my back, but I don't care. No one messes with Nick's little sister.

Chapter Four

From: Nick.Hoffman@us.gov.org
To: Beth.Hoffman@mymail.com
Dear Burpie,
Yeah, you hate that name too. I remember holding you on my shoulder and you vomiting milk down my back and ruining my favorite chick magnet T-shirt. Doesn't matter that I was nine, the chicks loved that shirt. It's funny how those memories are so important here. War sucks and the only thing keeping my head on straight are thoughts of you and talking to Rack. You know, the guy I want you to marry? The only guy who can protect you from your crazy self and make you happy. I think he's half in love with you from the stories I tell him about your wild ways. He also loves talking about his family. He has four brothers and awesome parents. For such a badass, he's a family man. When we're out of this hellhole you'll meet him and understand.
Your chick magnet brother,
Nick

* * * *

Beth
Angelo paces in front of me fisting his hands slowly, and a pulse ticks beside his eye. I never take my gaze off him. If he hits me, I want to see it coming and protect the baby. The severe beatings stopped once the pregnancy showed, but Angelo still has no problem striking my face. I don't want to fall if it happens.

"You are to stay out of the men's rooms. You don't want to see what I do to them if you go into one again."

Of course he knows the threat against his men is far too real to me. I was a blubbering fool months ago when he pulled me from the room with the man he killed. "I'm sorry," I say meekly. "I don't know how much longer I'll be able to take walks and I didn't want to miss one due to the weather. It was foolish of me."

He studies me, his face growing redder with anger. *Act meek, act meek,* I say inside my head. I can't allow a spark of rebellion to show. Angelo believes he can read a person by the look in their eyes. I've become very good at hiding how I truly feel.

"You won't need something warmer regardless of the weather. You're confined to the house until my son is born," he says flatly.

My hand trembles as I bring it to my stomach. I'm doing everything I can to keep from crying in front of him. He loves my tears and gains satisfaction from my fear. I don't bother arguing, I just rub my belly and accept the punishment.

"If you need exercise, I would think walking through the house would be enough." His look of disgust says far more than his biting words. He hasn't touched me since my belly grew round. I thank God for it every day. He brings women to the house and struts them in front of me. He's so arrogant he thinks I care.

I hate him.

I want him to die.

I won't give up, and when the time is right, I'll fight him until there is no breath left in my body. Hoffmans do not go gentle into that good night.

My brother's loss hits me again. He fought to the very end and I will do the same. I miss him so much. He would have killed Angelo. Imagining the death of my baby's father makes me a wicked person, but I don't care. There is no way my child can grow up with this monster.

I need Rack to help me out of this mess. I can only hope he researches Angelo before he charges in. If he charges in. A thought flashes through my brain—he could have a new phone number by now. "May I be excused so I may lie down?" I ask softly.

Angelo waves me away and turns his back.

I walk slowly to my room trying not to panic. What if I dialed a number that now belongs to someone else and that person texts back? I inhale deeply. I need to stop borrowing trouble. If I keep this level of anxiety up, I'll deliver the baby a month early. *Calm and controlled,* I remind myself.

* * * *

Dinner is a nightmare. Angelo has two lady friends joining him tonight. He doesn't bother introducing me. He fawns over the women and they laugh at his sexually inappropriate jokes. I ignore their curious looks. I'm accustomed to Angelo's behavior. At first I thought he was trying to make me jealous. That's not it, though. I'm a possession and he wants me to know he controls every aspect of my life. He would kill these women without a thought and enjoy it.

The dining room, like the rest of the ranch house, is a glamorous facade to hide the evil that lurks inside. The light fixture hanging over the long, black, lacquered table is worth more than I made in a year as a secretary.

I cut off the thoughts of my other life and stare down at my plate. I'm always hungry and even with the dreadful company, I eat every tasteless bite. With a disgusted glance at my empty plate, Angelo dismisses me from the room. I can't get out quick enough. One of the women was on her knees giving Angelo a blow job while we ate. The slurps made it hard to keep the food down.

I close my bedroom door behind me and hold back a scream. I'm too close to the edge tonight and I'm barely functioning. I wash up in the bathroom, hating the decor that gives the entire ranch a lifeless quality. Black and white with crystal accents throughout the entire home almost take away my ability to breathe. I crawl into bed. It's only a little after seven but I'm exhausted. I rest my hand on my belly. The baby rolls and I smile sadly, holding back tears that never seem to end.

"I'm sorry you won't have a father," I whisper into the dark room. "I'll be everything you need, I promise."

The baby settles down and I try to fall asleep even knowing I'll be up in a few hours to pee. My sleepy brain flitters to Rack and the day I met him. He stood too close, he smelled too good, and his haunted eyes went clear to my soul. Will he even want to help me? I can't stop the tears that slip silently down my face and soak the pillow.

I desperately need help or I wouldn't have called him and placed him in danger. How do I live with myself if he comes after me and something happens to him? Eventually I fall into an exhausted sleep.

Chapter Five

Rack

The firepower I have in the Jeep forces me to abide by speed laws. I push it when I can, long desolate roads where I can see car lights in the distance. I pull over twice and doze for thirty minutes having learned the art of catnapping in the military. It keeps me alert. About fifteen hours into the trip, the weather takes a drastic turn. I hate the fucking cold and my thin Arizona blood isn't happy. I'm in jeans and a light cotton T-shirt. My flak jacket is in the trunk. It has no sleeves but the Kevlar will help keep me warm when I put it on. For now, the Jeep's heater does the trick.

I try to mentally block the pain from my wound. The stitches pull and even with the shitload of antibiotics shot into me, it feels like my side is on fire. I've survived worse injuries and continued fighting—this is no different. It's better to dwell on the chill in the air. I'm a complete pussy when it comes to the cold.

Rain hits at the Montana state line. Camp Springs is two hours northeast of Billings. The rain continues in a steady downpour. The landscape changes to denser trees as I drive into the higher elevation. I honestly haven't concentrated much on my surroundings until now. I'm thirty minutes from Beth's location. I've spent twenty something hours thinking of her and running endless scenarios through my head, so I'm ready for all situations during her extraction.

Beth. I see her through her brother's eyes. During my final tour of Afghanistan, where I met Nick, there were long hours with nothing to do. We were always tense in between missions wanting the fight and hating the wait. We talked. Some men spoke about their sweethearts or wives. I talked about my brothers and parents. Nick talked about his baby sister. He essentially raised her alone because of his mother's illness. His pride came through in every word. I was never much for laughter. That changed when Nick told stories about Beth's escapades. He would wrap me in his memories and I would swear they were almost my own. I come from a close family and having someone with their own deep ties to a sibling made me feel at home. Nick's memories of Beth easily flow through my mind in between the loose plan I've come up with to rescue her.

First, I need to scout the property. The satellite images were good but nothing replaces eyes on the target. Before I head in guns blazing, I need proof of life. If Beth isn't alive, I'll blow the entire fucking ranch up and kill everyone but Angelo. The thought of Angelo touching Beth has me gripping the steering wheel until my knuckles turn blue. If he's hurt her or God forbid killed her, his death will be slow and painful. I'll keep the fucker alive for weeks peeling the skin from his bones, strip by bloody strip.

I turn off the main road fifteen minutes away and find a good spot to hide the Jeep. The dense foliage will keep it hidden from most eyes. There are about six hours of daylight remaining. I'm heading in as soon as it's dark. I eat two protein bars and down a bottle of water before slipping low in the seat and closing my eyes. The temperature drops without the Jeep's heater. There's a Mylar emergency blanket packaged in a pocket of the flak jacket but I don't bother with it. I can take the cold. I can, I will myself while shivering into needed sleep.

* * * *

Five hours later, I load the flak jacket with everything from C4 to hand grenades. My gear belt holds two handguns with another strapped to my ankle. I carry six magazines of extra ammo for the handguns and four extended mags for the M27, which I sling over my shoulder.

When the sun disappears, I head through the soggy forest terrain and try to ignore the temperature drop. It's summer for fuck's sake. There's a light drizzle and even with gloves my hands are freezing. I'm taking Beth to a warmer climate whether she wants it or not. I'll slay dragons for her as long as they're closer to the southern hemisphere. I start a slow jog and my body heats. I clear my mind of everything but my objective and go into survival mode.

The trees thin and I notice lights over the next ridge. I crawl up the hill and look down into a large valley. The ranch house is in the center of the cleared property. No cover. Using binoculars, I zero in on outside cameras. I'll need to take the power out. Chances are good they have a backup generator, but it will take time to start. Everything needs to be timed perfectly. There's a barn that I can place explosives in and detonate with my phone. For Beth, I'm willing to sacrifice any animals. This is my only shot at getting her out alive. I turn the binoculars to the upstairs windows looking for a sign of her. Ten minutes pass and still nothing.

The ranch house isn't huge but knowing her general location will increase the chance of reaching her and getting her out safely. There are three upstairs windows. Two have open curtains and one drawn. There's a balcony off one of the rooms with double doors. My guess is it's the master suite. That's where I'm going in. Now I just need to stay alive and not freeze to death over the next few hours.

Monitoring the windows for Beth helps keep my mind off the cold. I've been in worse situations but truthfully a hot bed of coals would be more pleasant to lie on. My pants and shirt are soaked from the rain and my body temperature is dropping.

I watch two guards make rounds. Some very bad men want Angelo dead. He's playing it safe. Not safe enough, however. Two hours later, I catch movement from the bedroom with the pulled curtain. *Come on, Beth, let me know you're there and okay.* My silent prayer is answered when the covering moves aside and she peers out for a few seconds. It's only a flash, but I would recognize the outline of her face anywhere. I still have the picture of her that her brother kept in his wallet. It survived the blast that took him out and I've kept it all this time.

An hour later, I head to the powerline pole that provides electricity to the ranch. I climb the pegs in the wood utility pole and place a leg over the cross beam. I need to be above the cable I cut so it falls free and doesn't hit me. I feel around the flak jacket for a small hand-grip cable cutter located in a back pocket. The only positive right now is that the rain stopped about thirty minutes ago. I place my hands on the rubber guard of the cutters and start working the cable coming from the transformer. The electrical current from the transformer is lower voltage and there's less chance of electrocution if I'm hit. The 240 volts will knock me off the wire and most likely culminate in a broken neck. When the cable snaps, a few sparks fly as it drops to the ground and the power goes out. I shimmy down the pole thankful for the gloves. I flip the night goggles over my eyes and start running. My destination is the barn. I make it to the side of the aluminum structure and stop to listen. I hear voices from the direction of the house. I slide around the side of the barn and check the door. It's unlocked and I slip inside. I remove the goggles and pull out a small flashlight with a red light setting that gives off a muted glow. There are two vehicles inside. A truck is outside, which I'll take care of after I've wired the barn. I work quickly and secure the C4 to the vehicles. I place a small detonator that I can control remotely with an app on my cell phone—the shit you can do with technology these days is unreal.

I work under the vehicles in case someone enters the barn. When I'm done, I check outside. I hear the generator, but it's controlling only about half the power required to light up the house. The truck is twenty yards away. I'm about to make a run for it, when two men walk outside.

"Check the power pole. The transformer probably blew. I've called the power company," one of the men says to the other.

"I'm sure boss is shittin' his pants," the other guy says with a laugh. "What the fuck does he expect to happen in Montana?"

Both are carrying rifles, and my plan to take out the truck is shot to hell. If the man checking the transformer knows anything about how it works, he'll know the line has been cut. Things are about to get interesting. I'm taking a chance that the cameras aren't running, but it's all I have. One of the men drives away in the truck and the other heads back inside.

I run for the house as soon as the front door closes. There's a tree near the balcony, which is how I'm getting to the second floor. I scramble up the tree and remove the gloves to make the jump from the tree to the balcony. My adrenaline is high and the cold isn't affecting me right now. It's a five foot jump. I grab the bottom iron rail, swing back, and bring my leg up. When I'm over the rail, I maneuver into the shadows. A few stitches in my wound ripped out in the jump and fire lights up my side. I ignore it and fit the silencer to the modified threaded barrel of the Glock. If all hell breaks loose, I'll go to the M27. I take slow steady breaths.

It's time to play.

Chapter Six

From: Nick.Hoffman@us.gov.org
To: Beth.Hoffman@mymail.com
Dear Bethiboop,
Rough times here and we had a close call yesterday. I worry about you if something happens to me. I know you're all grown up but it's important to me that you have someone great to spend your life with and care for you. Rack is that guy! He's made for you. If the unthinkable happens, you can rely on him. He will get you out of any scrapes you find yourself in. I promise. The man is a daredevil with the luck of a leprechaun. Your children will be the hellions you deserve.
Your melancholy brother,
Nick

* * * *

Beth

No lady friends visited Angelo tonight, so he concentrates on me. With methodical precision, he cuts his meat and takes small bites while watching me. He finally wipes his mouth and places his fork on his plate. "You've gained weight. It's not healthy for my child."

I'm pregnant for fuck's sake. It's not healthy to be a beanpole in your eighth month. I keep this to myself. "I think walking helped keep the water weight down." I actually have no idea if this is true, but I'll go stir crazy trapped in the house for the next month. "My ankles are swollen and I'm sure the rest of me is too." I say this as subserviently as possible. It was a miserable day all around. I thought about my brother, my choices...Rack. He isn't coming. It hasn't been long enough for him to get here, but that doesn't matter. It was a long shot and the chance he got the text, arranged to rescue me, and is on his way is nothing but a pipe dream. Depression pulls the walls in making the house feel small.

"You think to manipulate me by claiming lack of exercise?" he demands, startling me from my gloomy thoughts.

"I'm sorry," I lower my eyes before lifting them again. "I didn't sleep well last night. I'm eating the food provided for me, but I'll cut back."

His chair scrapes against the hardwood floor. He rises slowly. My heartrate accelerates as he walks up behind me. He lifts the hair from my neck and leans in. "Your attitude needs an adjustment," he whispers, his hot breath sliding over my skin. His large hand moves around to my throat and he tilts my head in an uncomfortable angle. "I look forward to giving you the discipline you so obviously need." His hand tightens and he cuts off my air. I can't help myself and lift my hands to his. He eases the pressure. "When you no longer incubate my child, you will be very, very sorry."

As threats go, it's a good one. I've been sorry since the day I discovered what a monster he truly is. Tears slide down my cheeks. I can't hold them back. I drop my hands to my lap. His hand moves from my throat to my breast. He squeezes one nipple and pain erupts. I inhale sharply and fight jerking away.

"You will never feed my child. These will be mine. I promise I have wonderful plans for them." He releases me and moves my half-eaten plate toward the center of the table. "You've had enough. Return to your room." He pulls out my chair like a proper gentleman. A devil. *The* devil.

My days are numbered after the baby arrives. I've known it, but Angelo's actions tonight prove it. He'll even deny me feeding my child. I walk slowly to my room holding back the sobs collected in my throat until I close the door behind me. I sink to the floor and cry into my hands. It's not a pretty cry. I bawl my eyes out until snot runs down my face and I'm forced to heft myself up and make my way to the bathroom for tissue. If Angelo saw me struggling to get up like this, he would never feed me again.

I want to die.

The baby kicks and more despair swamps me. I head to the window and move the curtain aside gazing into the darkness. I have nowhere to go. No one to help me. If I kill Angelo myself, will his men spare my child or kill me straight out? I can't risk it and even if I did I probably wouldn't succeed. The curtain slips from my fingers and I crawl into bed. I wish a good night's sleep would make tomorrow better, but I know that won't happen.

This princess will never escape her tower. At least not alive.

Chapter Seven

Rack

The curtain of the master bedroom is partially open. I check inside the dark room and see no movement. I take out my phone and pull up the app to blow the barn. With the phone in one hand and my finger hoovering over the control, I lift the gun. My finger presses down and I swing the butt of the gun against the glass as the explosion rocks the balcony. I'm in the house before flying debris settles.

I'm about to enter the hallway when a voice yells up the stairs and running feet move closer. "Lock her in the damn room and get your ass back here."

I move behind the door and watch one of the guards run past. I don't move as he locks the door to the room where they're keeping Beth. I wait for him to charge back down the stairs before I run to the door he just secured. I remove a metal wedge from one of my vest pockets and put it against the door to pry it into the lock. The door snaps open without much force. The room's dark and I flash the tactical light on the Glock at the bed. Empty.

"Beth," I say as quietly as possible.

She runs from the entrance of what I assume is the bathroom and throws her arms around me. "Rack, oh my God, Rack."

She's crying and I need her to pull herself together. What can one quick hug hurt, though? I gather her into my arms and inhale the scent I remember from our one and only meeting. What I don't remember is her expanded waistline. With my free hand, I force her back and look down.

"Fuck," I say when I see the size of her stomach.

In the very faint light from my tactical light I watch her hands go to her belly. "I'm sorry, I'm so sorry," she cries.

I'm not sure what she's apologizing for. Her pregnancy fucks up my escape plans and my brain is moving a hundred miles an hour to come up with a new plan. "Whose child is it?" Her lips tremble and I think she sees my question as an accusation. "Will Angelo shoot you and risk killing the baby?" I try again.

She shakes her head, but I see so much guilt in her eyes. I pull her back against me and whisper into her ear, "How far can you make it on foot?"

Her fingers grip my vest. "As far as I need to. If I don't get out of here, I'm dead as soon as the baby comes."

"Three miles. I need three miles from you." She nods against my shoulder. "Dress quickly and put your best running shoes on, we're getting out of here."

She releases me and moves away. She turns slightly and I see the full girth of her belly. This won't be easy. She has the blood of her brother running through her veins, though. It means she's one tough cookie. I won't tell her that our chances of escape have narrowed to nothing. I need her to give me everything she has and then give more. I turn to the door and push it almost shut and check the hallway. I move to the windowsill and quickly rig another explosive charge. If we make it to the downstairs backdoor, I need another disruption.

"I'm ready," she says over my shoulder.

I set the detonator and turn. She's dressed in black—the pants do nothing to hide her enormous belly. I check her feet and the deck shoes are not as encouraging as the rest of her outfit but they'll do.

"You need a coat or jacket."

"I don't have one."

We're in the same boat. "Stay behind me. My vest is bullet-proof and will work against hand guns. If I say run, you run. If I say give yourself up, you do it. Understand?" I order.

Her tears are gone and there's no fear in her expression. I see the Hoffman perseverance her brother had. She nods and I give her a chin lift.

"Let's rock 'n roll," I say because that was her brother's favorite expression and I need him to watch out for Beth while I take care of everything else. I check the hall again and place her hand on the back of my belt. "Give a tug if you see anyone behind us," I tell her.

"Okay," she whispers.

I move out of the room aware of the woman I'm protecting. A very...pregnant...woman. Not a single scenario I imagined on the way here included this. My resolve to kill Angelo increases. He'll never give up looking for his child and his death is the only outcome that makes perfect sense. She won't be able to make it down the tree, and the low lights controlled by the generator leave the stairs fully exposed. There's no choice. We hug the wall as I take the stairs one at a time so she doesn't fall.

"Which way to the back door?" I ask quietly.

"Hallway on your left." Her voice is hushed but rock solid.

I push her in front of me so my back is to the front door. "Down," I say when the door opens. I fire at the man who enters and hear Beth make a strangled noise when he drops. The guy was young and not Angelo. "Go," I tell her. There's a shout from out front.

I reach over Beth when we hit the back door and I unlock it. I move around her and check both directions. There's a small bush against one side of the house. I quickly move to it with her holding my belt again. "Crawl behind the bush and stay put."

"But..."

I don't have time for gentleness and unclench her hand from my belt. "Do what I fucking say," I hiss. She drops to her knees and crawls behind the bush. I hug the outside wall and inch toward the side of the house so I can see what's happening out front. Headlights approach from the road. It's the truck from earlier. The driver slams on the brakes and the truck slides several feet. He's about twenty yards from the front door.

Someone yells "cover me" from an unknown direction. The man in the truck gets out with his rifle at ready. The hidden man runs for the truck. It's Angelo. I studied his face from a picture I found on the Internet. I could take him but I might not get them both. "Go get her," Angelo yells at the man with the rifle.

I pull out the phone and take that option out of the equation by detonating the C4. The windows blow and fire spills from the room. Angelo stares for several seconds before both men jump in the truck and it takes off. Now I need to get Beth to the Jeep. We need to be as far from here as possible. I move back and help her stand.

"Angelo thinks you're dead. It buys us some time."

"He's not dead?" she asks shakily.

"No."

She closes her eyes and I can't help but wonder if she has feelings for him. I don't like it. Her eyes open and lock with mine. "After the baby's born, I'll kill him myself."

That settles that.

I don't tell her that Angelo is all mine. Beth's brother would have it no other way. "We're moving out. Tell me if you need me to slow down." I don't have her hold my belt. She needs both hands for balance and to break her fall if she goes down. I don't see Angelo coming back tonight. He'll gather more men, which could take a day or two. Right now it's the cold climate I'm worried about. The temperature is dropping fast and neither of us is dressed for the outdoors.

I set out at a slower pace than I planned. Beth is breathing hard around the half mile point. I steer her to a fallen tree and take her hand to help her sit. Her fingers are freezing. I forgot about the gloves. I remove them from my vest and push them over her trembling fingers. "You okay?"

"I'm good, give me two minutes."

"If we stop for longer than that, your body temperature will drop. We need to keep going."

"I only asked for two minutes," she snaps. Her hand goes to her belly while she tries to catch her breath.

I'm completely out of my element. "Is the baby coming?"

Her startled eyes lift. "No, dummy, she's just kicking," she snaps between huffs of air.

Damn, my face flushes. "How far along are you?" I think this is a normal question for pregnant women.

"Eight months. I have a month to go and the baby is sitting tight until then. We'll make it."

"I know we will. You ready to move?" I place my hand out and she takes it.

"Lead the way."

Chapter Eight

From: Nick.Hoffman@us.gov.org
To: Beth.Hoffman@mymail.com
Dear Delusional Beth,
This Kevin guy is not for you. You need to trust your older, wiser
brother on this. Kevin has no idea the spirit you carry inside you. He
can't. I can tell by your emails that he's a stodgy prick. And yes you
read that right. I don't need to meet him. You need to meet Rack.
He'll blow all thoughts of this other man out of your head.
Your wiser, older brother,
Nick

* * * *

Beth
Rack came for me. A man I've met one time. A man Nick said was
the best person on the planet. I should have had more faith in my
brother.

My stomach cramps and I dig my fingers into my side. I
know it's not the baby coming. I should have exercised more while I
had the chance. Even with the pace Rack sets, I'm freezing and my
teeth are chattering. I know he's moving much slower than he wants
to. I put one foot in front of the other and refuse to stop. Ignoring my
frozen toes, the ache in my side, and the terror living in the center of
my chest is another matter.

Rack halts after another hundred yards or so and starts
removing his gear. I have no idea what's up, but I'm too winded to
ask. There's no place to sit this time. He rests the items he's carrying

carefully on the ground next to a tree. He shrugs out of the vest and places it around my shoulders.

"Slip your arms in," he says when I just stand there in a stupor.

The vest is heavy but warm from his body heat. He takes off one of my gloves and checks my fingers. "They're good," I say between teeth chatters.

"I expect you to be honest with me. If we need to stop, say so." His voice isn't harsh, just matter of fact.

I tilt my head back and look into his dark eyes. He's at least six inches taller than I am. The moon casts enough light to see strength, honor, and sacrifice in the green orbs. Nick's were the same way. I absorb the strength of Rack's gaze and I know whatever happens, this man will give his life for mine. Normally this would upset me but I have the baby to think of. "I need to sit down," I tell him truthfully.

He leads me to a tall tree a few feet away. He places his back to the tree, turns me, and wraps me in his arms. He sinks to the ground taking me awkwardly with him. His arms adjust and he situates me slightly so I'm cradled against his chest. He pulls his rifle closer and then tightens his arms a bit.

"We'll rest for thirty minutes and then move again. I need to know if you get too cold."

"I thought it was better to keep moving," I whisper against his warmth. I swear my entire messed up world fades away. I never want to leave the safety of his arms.

"You need a break. I promise to keep you warm for thirty minutes. Now close your eyes and rest."

I'm exhausted and figure my slow loops around Angelo's property did little in the way of keeping me fit. Of course the larger my stomach got, the slower I walked. Stupid really, I could have pushed it more and been prepared to escape.

I snuggle a little closer. "Tell me something about my brother and I'll rest." I miss Nick so bad it hurts. This man knew my brother in ways I never did. My brother was always a badass and I so badly want to hear the stories. Rack remains quiet and I don't think he's going to answer.

"Your brother talked about you all the time. He said you were superwoman."

I laugh and sink further into Rack. "He called me supergirl all the time."

"He was very proud of you."

I catch the sob that's working its way up my throat. "He raised me, you know."

"He told me. You were what? Twelve when your mother died?"

"Nine and he was eighteen but he raised me long before that. Mom was always sick. She had MS. Our father left when we were young. I still don't know what happened to him. One day he was there and the next he wasn't. I was six then. Nick just took over. He even found odd jobs and supplemented Mom's Social Security. He was always just there, bigger than life, taking on the world."

We both stop talking. I didn't mean to do this. I know Rack still hurts over the death of my brother. I saw it the day I met him. He feels responsible and it showed in his eyes. Nick would hate that. He thought of Rack the same way he thought of me. His protective instincts were always in overdrive. My brother has been my hero for as long as I can remember, and now he's given me another hero.

"He loved you," Rack says softly.

"I know."

We stay there for what seems like only minutes, when Rack shakes me out of a light sleep. "We need to move."

I stiffen and realize I'm unable to move. "I can't get off you," I say in mortification.

"You don't weigh that much," he says with a laugh.

How he gets his legs beneath him and lifts me is a miracle that I don't want to repeat. He lowers my legs until my feet plant firmly on the ground. I sway and he settles me with a hand on my shoulder. Without his body warmth, I quickly grow cold again. He must be freezing. "I don't think I can walk far with the vest." I shrug out of it and he lifts it from my hands and puts it on. He picks up his gear and secures everything in place. The cold seeps beneath my clothes.

"Come on, walking will help. The Jeep's two miles away."

I hold my stomach when we start moving. I step carefully, aware that falling won't help. My feet are frozen and I worry about frostbite. The thin socks I'm wearing are no help at all. Two miles. I can make it. We'll be fine once we reach Rack's Jeep.

I know we haven't gone a half mile when I almost trip over a branch. Rack gathers me into his arms, lifts me, and keeps walking. "Put me down, you can't carry me."

"Stop wiggling and making it harder. We're both freezing." His tone is hard. It's an order.

Orders don't sit well with me, but he's right. We need to find the Jeep. I clench my hands into the vest under his arms. Leaning against the vest is not nearly as comfortable as wearing it. Pocket-y things stick into me. I'll be damned if I complain.

Rack carries me and my extra belly weight like it's nothing. At least during the first mile. His breath comes in stronger gasps as he continues walking. I'm almost about to insist he put me down again, when he stops.

"The Jeep is up ahead. I want to check it out before getting you situated." He removes the handgun from his holster and hands it to me. It no longer has the suppressor on it. Nick was a gun fanatic and taught me well. I pull the slide back and realize I can't see if there's one in the chamber.

"It's loaded and ready to go. You have twelve in the mag and one in the chamber." He doesn't question that I know what I'm doing when it comes to guns.

"Hurry back," I tell him.

He nods, pulls the rifle around, and disappears into the forest. I place my back to a tree like he did earlier, though I don't attempt to sit. Keeping the gun securely in my hand, I wrap my arms around myself and listen for strange noises.

The trees rustle with the slight breeze that's making it even colder. It should be cold enough to keep animals in their dens. I don't notice the normal critter noises I would expect. A few minutes later the crunch of a branch makes me move the gun and turn slightly to the side.

"You're good, it's me. Come on, I started the engine so it will be warm when you get inside."

I want to laugh and cry at the same time. Angelo might not be dead but Rack got me out of there and now my baby has a chance.

Chapter Nine

Rack

I lift her into the passenger seat of the Jeep. It's barely warmed but anything is better than outside. I have the Mylar blanket ready to go and tuck it in around her. I didn't want it shining through the trees while we headed to the Jeep in case Angelo circled back looking for the person who blew up the house.

She's shivering. I shut the door as quickly as possible and move to the driver's side. I throw the Jeep in gear and pull onto the road. I chose this spot so I could move forward and hit the road in case we were in a hurry. With everything involved, the extraction went good. Maybe too good.

Beth moves her hands to the vents to heat them. I'm as cold as fuck but hey, I'm tough. I refuse to act like a pussy in front of her. I head back to the long stretch of road I came in on and see no vehicle lights in front or behind us. I head east at the intersection. I don't have a plan that involves a pregnant woman. At least not yet. I'll check my phone when I'm sure we're out of danger and see if Moon has responded to the information I left him. If he's smart, he'll stay out of this and Moon is a very smart man.

"You okay?" I ask Beth. She's deceptively quiet. I need her communicating any problems besides the obvious one of being frozen almost solid.

"Better," she replies with trembling lips that I can just make out within the Jeep's dark interior.

"Push back the seat if you need to. We'll be on the road for hours."

"Umm," she says followed by, "never mind."

"That won't cut it," I tell her. "You tell me what you need and I'll take care of it."

She groans and I'm about to push again when she says, "Bathroom. I need to go frequently."

"Like right now?" I ask, astonished.

"I'll make it another thirty minutes," she replies stubbornly.

Thirty minutes isn't good. I doubt we'll find a bathroom before that. I also don't want to stop at a gas station or anywhere that might have video cameras. I'm not dealing with just Angelo. I'm dealing with his father's organization, which has a long reach. I check the clock on the dash and drive for twenty minutes. There's a turn off and I pull in and head off the main road for a short distance.

"What are you doing?" Beth asks grumpily.

"You'll need to take advantage of Mother Nature. We can't stop at a restroom and chance cameras..."

She cuts me off and says, "Have you seen the size of me? I can't squat somewhere and go," she huffs indignantly.

"You can and you will. No other choice. I'll help."

I park the Jeep and she throws her door open. "Stay right where you are. I'll do this myself if it kills me."

I do my best not to smile. "Would toilet paper help?" I ask before she slams the door.

"Yes, you jerk."

I have sympathy, I really do, but she's damn cute and it's hard to hide my smile. I open my door and head to the back of the Jeep, where I have emergency supplies. A small roll of biodegradable paper is in the kit. I place the roll in her outstretched hand. "You need help. Let me assist you. I promise I'll close my eyes. Your modesty is safe with me."

"I'd rather die," she snaps and walks off. I turn around and watch for passing cars. A few minutes later I hear, "Rack, I need your help."

I head in the direction her voice came from. She's leaning against a tree. "Come on," I tell her. "It's not that bad."

"That's what you think," she sniffs. "What if I had to hold your dick so you could go?"

My dick twitches at the thought. I've imagined her doing just that. Okay, not so I can take a piss, but having her fingers wrapped around me is one of my favorite fantasies. Her damn brother started this mess from his nightly stories.

I move behind her, spread my legs to either side of hers, and place my hands beneath her arms. "Pull down your pants and squat. I'll ease you down and keep my eyes closed while doing it." I shut my eyes and concentrate on the movement of her body.

"What if I piss on your boots?" she all but sobs.

"They'll wash. Come on, it's cold."

"I can't believe I'm doing this. I hate being pregnant. The indignities keep mounting," she whines. She shifts and I hear the slide of her pants going down. I step back slightly and lean down allowing her to bend at her knees. "The doctor Angelo hired to examine me was a creep. He did perv-y things and Angelo watched." She stops talking and the sound of her peeing fills the night.

"I'll kill the doctor and Angelo for you."

"Angelo is mine," she sasses.

"Okay, I'll take the doctor." Over my dead body will she kill Angelo but now's not the time to argue about it.

Her hands shift and I clue in that she's wiping herself. "Can you lift me a little?" I lift her and turn so she's not standing in the wet spot. I help her stand upright and she readjusts her clothes. "You can release me. Thank you." Her teeth are beginning to chatter again.

I move to the side and take her hand. "Come on, let's get you to the Jeep where it's warmer."

I tuck her back into her seat with the Mylar blanket. "Get some sleep and let me know when you need to go again."

"I will. At least it shouldn't be as mortifying the next time."

I don't mention her need to do other business. I feel another argument coming on for that one. I reach back and hand her a bottle of water. "I know you don't want to go as often but you need to stay hydrated." She takes the water and twists off the top. After she takes a few sips she hands it to me. I take a pull and place it in the cup holder between us. "Sleep," I say softly.

"Okay, but I'll drive when you need to sleep."

I don't answer. The sun will be up in a few hours. I want to clear Wyoming and get into Colorado before stopping.

Chapter Ten

From: Nick.Hoffman@us.gov.org
To: Beth.Hoffman@mymail.com
Dear Stubborn Beth,
You're not listening. This guy is bad for you. You'll be bored within a year if you marry him. I know he hasn't asked yet but I can read between the lines. You can't marry him without me there, so I may never come home. I know in your stubbornness you will react irrationally if I try to tell you what to do. You have always been the most obstinate baby/girl/woman I know. I'm asking you to take things slow and wait.
Your equally stubborn brother,
Nick

* * * *

Beth

I wake up cramped and needing to pee again. The Jeep stops moving and I peer out the window. We're at a rest stop. Rack reaches into the back seat and hands me a small travel pouch.

"Make it quick. The toothbrush is mine, use it. I'll give you five minutes. Leave everything behind if I tell you to move. I don't expect trouble but we need to be prepared."

I cover my mouth. "My breath is that bad?"

He smiles and I think my heart stops. He has dimples. "No," he says and shakes his head. "I just know my mother would want to brush her teeth."

There can't be a more perfect man on the planet. He's as far from Angelo and the criminal world as you can get. My brother was right in telling me to contact Rack. Of course, I don't think my brother was ever wrong about anything. I would say joining the military was not a wise choice because it got him killed. I can't, though, because Nick had a sense of duty and fighting for this country was part of it.

I stop daydreaming when Rack's brow furrows. It makes little difference that the sun is coming over the horizon, it's cold. I hustle, which means a fast waddle into the bathroom. I do my business thankful Rack doesn't need to hold me while I do it. I glance into the metal mirror, which misshapes my face and still doesn't hide my swollen eyes or my hair sticking up in odd places. The travel bag is a bathroom kit and has a comb but no hairbrush. I wash my face and hands and then move to the hand dryer to dry myself. The heat feels good. I don't mind brushing my teeth with Rack's toothbrush. It's kind of sexy. I don't care if I'm the size of a barn. Sexy is sexy and Rack is the definition. Why didn't I call him after breaking it off with Kevin?

Shit. What if Rack is in a relationship or married? He doesn't wear a ring but that means nothing in today's world. I don't know why I'm even having these thoughts. I'm pregnant with another man's child. If Rack is single and desperate, I still wouldn't be on his list. I leave the ladies' room after combing my hair and hand him the bathroom kit.

"Your turn. I'll keep watch."

He hands me the handgun after I'm situated in the front seat of the Jeep. He rolls the window down. "I'll be quick. Yell if someone pulls up."

I wrap the silver blanket around me. I can't remember what they're called. I have pregnancy brain, PN for short, or at least that's what it feels like. PN makes me cry, forget the simplest things, and makes me think I need to pee every hour. I rub my hand over my stomach.

"I told you we would be okay. Your mom doesn't give false promises," I whisper. That's so far from the truth it's ridiculous, but I need my baby to understand she's safe.

Rack is out in half the time it took me. I watch him stride to the Jeep. And oh man he can stride. He has the lethal walk of a predator. Add in bulging muscle and badass tats and Rack is extra yummy. Pregnancy has had another effect on me. I swear I've been horny since day one. I haven't had sex with anything other than my fingers in six months. I fight back a groan and must make some small distressed noise because Mr. Lethal gives me a quick look.

"Everything okay?" he asks.

"Perfect," I reply and try to wipe my last thoughts from my mind.

He hands me a brown bag which he pulled from the trunk before we left the rest stop. "Energy bars and fruit. Eat what you need." He puts the Jeep in gear and pulls out.

I'm starving. I peer into the bag and remove one of the bars. I hand it to him. "I'll eat one if you eat the other."

He takes it without arguing. The bag also holds an apple. I eat the bar first. "Do you have a knife?" I ask after the bar is gone and I pull out the apple.

"You're not using a knife while we're moving. Eat half and I'll take the rest when you're done."

"You're bossy, you know that?" I smile because I want him to smile back at me. Boy do I want him to smile back. I'm such a pathetic excuse for a pregnant woman.

He glances over and I think it's going to happen. Then his gaze drops to my stomach and he snaps his eyes back to the road. I can't imagine a woman in my condition causing any kind of flirtatious behavior in a man who looks like Rack. This stomach completely kills a mood, even an imaginary one. I can't believe I'm having any of these thoughts. Damn, I'm just losing my mind.

I eat part of the apple and cast covert glances his way while he drives. He's lickable sin. I want his lush mouth all over me. His brutally muscled arms wrapped around me and his...Oh, God I need to stop.

I take steady breaths to try to hide my crazy thoughts. I lean a little to the right in the seat and settle back, turned slightly so I can see him without it appearing so obvious. He has three tattooed crosses on the side of his throat and a full arm sleeve of beautiful artwork. Nick never mentioned Rack being an overly religious man but the crosses say differently. Again, he's as close to perfect as I can picture a man. I can't help wondering if there are more tats where I can't see. My body heats and I'm uncomfortably warm. I take my last bite of apple and chew slowly.

"Do you need to go again?" he asks me.

My face heats. I guess I was squirming just a bit. "No, I'm good. Here's your half of the apple."

"Eat it, I'm not hungry."

I pull the apple back and take another bite. I eat with one hand and rub my belly with the other. It's habit. The swirling over my stomach calms me. The desire doesn't leave, though. I'm a woman and even pregnancy can't ruin my fantasy.

"We'll get a room tonight and you can shower. I'll pick up some clothes for you to change into once we're settled in the room. Too many stores have cameras. I don't want you seen."

A shower sounds heavenly. I finish the apple and place the core in the bag. "Could we manage real food?"

His lip quirks and a hint of his smile shows. "What type of real food do you like?" he asks.

With his incredible body he probably exists on energy bars and protein drinks. I've been eating overcooked vegetables and bland meat for months. "Pizza, I crave pizza with everything on it." I expect a response similar to what Angelo would give me. What I get is Rack's full smile.

"Pizza it is."

I salivate over the thought of pizza and what his smile does to my insides. The baby kicks in pleasure even though she has no idea what pizza is. The tears come out of nowhere. It's been this way since I became pregnant—perfectly okay one minute and a sobbing mess the next. Rack jerks the Jeep off the road. He's out the door and at mine before I realize what's going on. He throws my door open, releases my seatbelt and has me in his arms. I hiccup between gasps for air while clenching his shirt.

"Shh," he whispers while rubbing my back. His muscled arms tighten and he's completely supporting my jelly legs with my extended belly plastered to the front of him. Everything I've been through pours out—the pain, the fear, the utter desolation. This man saved me. Saved my child. He doesn't even know us. We're nothing to him. His friend's sister. That's all. And he came through.

"Shh," he says repeatedly. He finally pushes me back in the seat and takes a knee on the ground. He picks up my hand and moves it to his chest. "You're safe." He wipes hair from my face where it's sticking to my tears. He uses his T-shirt to wipe the tears and snot. I'm such a basket case that I don't even care. At least not until a bubble blows from my nose and I snort.

"See, everything will be okay," he says with another heart-stopping smile.

"It's the baby. I never cry, but she makes me cry all the time," I say between hiccups.

"I don't know anything about babies or being pregnant. It helps when you tell me these things. I thought it was the pizza."

I manage a small giggle. "It was the pizza. Angelo monitored my food and made me eat healthy. No sugar and no damn pizza."

"Just another reason to kill him," he responds lightly but his eyes darken. "I'll pick up pizza and ice cream if you want?"

"A hot fudge sundae and I'll love you forever."

"I can manage that." He palms my cheek and tilts my face up a bit. "We'll find you someone special to love. He'll be a great father for your little girl."

I'm looking at someone special. All I've thought about for months was escaping and raising my child alone. I was totally off men. And now...now I want this man so bad it hurts. "She could be a he. I don't know but I was just kind of hoping for a girl. I didn't want a boy to turn out like his father." I sniff and tears well again.

Rack's fingers run beneath my eyes. "None of that. There's no way your baby will turn out like Angelo. There's too much of Nick in him or her."

I push forward so my cheek rests on his shirt. That's the nicest thing he could possibly say. I'm ready to start bawling again but manage to gain control. The buzz of a phone coming from behind me makes me jump.

"It's my cell," Rack says. "I turned it on at the rest stop." He pushes me gently back into my seat and fastens my seatbelt. His fingers glide across my belly as he adjusts it. My stomach doesn't seem to disgust him like it did Angelo. I was carrying the asshole's child and he never so much as ran a finger over my belly. Rack walks around his side and opens the back door. He checks the message while standing beside the car. "Fuck," he says and then walks to the front of the Jeep, slams his hand on the hood, and returns to his door. He gets in without looking at me. The hard set of his jaw makes me afraid to ask what's wrong. Before I got pregnant, before Angelo, I wouldn't have hesitated. Angelo turned me into a victim and I don't like it.

Rack pulls back out on the road. There's a bit more traffic now and I lean back and close my eyes. For now I'll continue being weak and let Rack handle whatever it is that's upset him. I'm exhausted from crying. My eyelids weigh too much and I can no longer fight the need to sleep.

Chapter Eleven

Rack

The sound of her soft snore fills the car. I glance at Beth and she's fast asleep. I shake my head. She's held up better than I expected or at least what I expected after I saw she was pregnant.

The son of a bitch controlled her food. My hands tighten on the steering wheel. I *will* kill the bastard. He's now first on my list and far in front of the last two men responsible for killing my brother. I haven't forgotten about the doctor who examined her either.

I picture each death in my head because that's better than picturing Beth in my arms. I want her. It may even be in the sick way Angelo wanted her. Possession is a powerful word. Possessive and obsessive both work. It began long before I met her in person. Nick started it. He got it in his head that I would marry her. He actually teased me about it non-stop. I was a different man back then. My marriage to Beth was settled as far as Nick was concerned.

It fit with the man I was before. I always wanted a large family and a house filled with laughter. I think that's why Nick and I hit it off. We were a lot alike in our love for family. I remember the email he received when Beth gushed over the man who became her fiancé. Nick hated him instantly. It didn't matter how many times I said I wasn't good enough for his baby sister. Nick had made up his mind.

"She's a handful, Rack. You're the only one who has a chance to keep her out of trouble." I'll never forget him saying that. It went against the military's unwritten oath that sisters were off limits to fellow soldiers.

Nick's blood dripping off my hands flashes through my mind. I've replayed his death a thousand times in my head. My hands fist the wheel tighter and my vision pinpoints taking me to the place inside my head that knows only killing. With a sharp breath, I gain control and turn my thoughts to the text message I received from Gomez.

Gimonde traced you.
Tell me what you need.

I did everything I could to keep Gimonde in the dark about my ties to Moon. Beth's text message on a compromised phone bothered me, though. Now Gomez is willing to help even though he knows the danger it brings down on Moon's organization. I can't go there unless it's our only hope.

The Jeep is in my name. Once I hit a city, every speed radar in the state will have record of me driving through. I'm sure the Gimonde family has my picture by now. They'll know I work for Moon, but they won't find out much after that. My records show Jones as my last name. I know it's not original. Doesn't matter. I've been Rack Jones since meeting Moon in Mexico. He made the arrangements for my name change to protect my family. My mother and father are still alive along with three of my brothers. I...I haven't seen my family since I turned my back on generations of law enforcement and took the criminal path. That was a few years ago. I regret nothing. Or at least I've told myself that. I won't deny I miss them.

I glance over at the sleeping woman again and know the police could not help her against the dangerous man she's involved with. She has me and I'll do everything I can to keep her safe.

I continue driving and avoid large towns, including Casper. Beth moves to more comfortable positions every hour or so but never comes fully awake. I pull into a small hotel in a midsize town near Boulder, Colorado, with a large discount store a few blocks away. I detected no speed or traffic light cameras, so I think we're good.

Beth groans when the car stops. "Please tell me there's a bathroom within five feet of the car," she says groggily.

"We're at the hotel and I need to check us in first. Stay here and I'll be right back."

She turns in my direction. "You don't understand. I need to go now."

"Too dangerous." I get out of the car and sprint into the hotel office. I'm back within five minutes.

Her hands cover her face and I know she's crying by the slight trembling in her shoulders. She glances up with a stricken expression. "I couldn't hold it. Oh, God, I'm sorry. The baby is sitting on my bladder and I couldn't hold it," she repeats.

I'm way too far out of my comfort zone with this. If she were a comrade in the military who peed himself, I could handle it. Shit literally happens when you're fighting for your life. I have no idea what to say to a pregnant woman with a baby sitting on her bladder. I put the Jeep in gear and drive around to the back of the hotel to locate our room. I pull in and walk around to help her out.

"I'm disgusting, I've ruined your seat," she cries.

I look at the seat and there's a small dark spot. "I can easily clean it. No worries. Let's get you inside and in the shower." I was good at making scared shitless rookie soldiers think I had everything under control. That ability is coming in handy right now.

I use the keycard, open the door, and usher her inside. After one last look around the parking lot, I follow her in. "Get in the shower and I'll grab my bag. I have a shirt that will do until I can buy you some clothes."

She doesn't acknowledge me, just walks into the bathroom and closes the door with a quiet click. If she were a man, I would easily make a joke about pissing over the spot on the seat to mark territory. There were times in trenches that all you could do was unzip and piss against the dirt in front of you. I rarely feel uncomfortable or out of my element. I get the job done by whatever means possible. That's completely changed. I am not trained for babies, tears, and squashed bladders.

I head outside and retrieve my bag along with the larger weapons bag. When I get back inside, I knock on the bathroom door and say, "I have a shirt for you."

"Come in and put it on the counter," she calls back. Her voice is stronger and she doesn't sound like she's crying.

I open the door and place the T-shirt next to the sink. The shower curtain is one of those heavy white things and I can see the outline of her body. Her extended belly holds my attention and then I notice her wet panties and bra hanging over the shower rod. I leave as quickly as I entered. If the bad things I've done don't send me to hell, getting a hard-on for a pregnant woman will.

I pace in the bedroom while she showers. I'm too wound up to lie down. I'd jack off if I could picture her like the first time I met her. I can't, though. The image locked in my head is of her with a rounded belly and a large beautiful ass. My dick gets harder. I hit the floor and start counting push-ups so my sane half doesn't kick the shit out of my filthy half for having these thoughts. The stitches in my side stretch and a few pop out. My side burns, but I don't stop pushing up and down.

Beth walks out of the bathroom at a hundred and fifty-six. No amount of push-ups on earth will ever get this sight out of my head. I quickly stand. The T-shirt barely covers the top of her thighs. Her legs are long and…perfect. My gaze travels upward to her round belly. After leaving my family, I cut off the thought of ever having children. Too dangerous in my line of work. The thought of Beth carrying my child knots my insides. She's as cute as a button. And beautiful. Her breasts fill the shirt above her belly. I meet her dark eyes so similar to her brother's. Red tinges her cheeks. A white towel holds her brown hair up and even that is adorable on her.

"You're beautiful," I say because it's true. Her hand goes to her stomach. It's what she does when she's nervous. I feel as if everything I say is coming from a clumsy ox. My brain goes cloudy around her. I tear my eyes away and pick up my handgun. The only way I can think straight right now is not to look at her. "I'm leaving you a gun." I place it on the night table between the two beds. "I'll be back as soon as possible. Don't open the door to anyone. Shoot first, ask questions later." I glance at her long enough to see her nod.

"I need your travel kit," she says without smiling. I have a feeling I'm giving off a creeper vibe.

"I'll grab it from the Jeep." I shouldn't have told her she's beautiful. If I don't get the hell out of the room, I'll say something else stupid.

Chapter Twelve

From: Nick.Hoffman@us.gov.org
To: Beth.Hoffman@mymail.com
Dear Darling Sister,
You heard me right and yes, I've been drinking. Rack and I drank too much tonight. His brother, back in the States, died yesterday and Rack's in a bad place. I'm worried for him. Worried he'll be reckless and get his ass shot. We move out early tomorrow morning and he shouldn't be going. He needs to return home but, like you, he's stubborn. Don't worry about me. I'm a badass. On a lighter note, I've convinced Rack he needs to marry you. Believe it or not it wasn't easy. Sooo, you need to kick this Kevin guy in the balls and move on. We'll be home in a few months and I'm hiring Rack to kidnap you and take you to a deserted island until you fall in love with each other. It's the only thing that will help him deal with his loss. I'm counting on you.
Your badass brother,
Nick

* * * *

Beth
I couldn't help noticing the growing bulge in Rack's pants before he walked out. Or the slightly larger one when he handed me the kit. Oh. My. God. He can't possibly think I'm beautiful, much less sexy. Can he? He was most likely thinking about a hot girlfriend or wife while I was showering. Damn, the bulge was large.

Seeing his hard muscles beneath a sweaty T-shirt doesn't exactly help my quirky pregnancy hormones either. What I wouldn't give to see him with no shirt. Hell, no clothing at all would give me a fantasy to remember for years.

My friends always said my brother was hot. I laughed because I just didn't see it. Handsome yes, hot as in sex…no, I just couldn't go there. Nick was a few inches shorter than Rack but he worked out and kept the women drooling. He was playfully conceited when he noticed women eyeing him.

"The babes love me, sis. It's this hot body that keeps them coming back for more."

I'd pantomime gagging and he'd laugh. Nick could get serious in a hurry, but my fondest memories are of him making me smile. I don't think Rack spends much time laughing or smiling. My brother wrote to me about Rack constantly and he tried his hardest to hook us up. Nick worried I would never find a man to settle down with. I had hopes and dreams—traveling around the world, meeting new people, making a difference. I met Kevin while working on a fund-raiser for children in Haiti. I thought Kevin had my same ambitions. I had absolutely no idea he wanted a political career, at least not until it was too late and I was in love with him. Kevin was quite passive aggressive. The last thing I wanted was a man who controlled me. Like most politicians, Kevin maneuvered around the truth and manipulated me. Now I realize how weak Kevin was. Fast forward to Angelo and it's obvious I'm a bad judge of character.

My brother was right about so many things, and I'm past the point of rejecting Rack. It doesn't matter that no man in his right mind would want a woman pregnant with another man's child. My heart is swelling with a ridiculous emotional attachment to Rack and I can't fight it.

After sleeping hours in the car I'm wide awake. The baby has decided to take a nap and even moved off my bladder, giving me some relief. My stomach growls from lack of food and I hope Rack hurries. I flip on the television, choose the bed most comfortable for watching TV, and lay on my side to watch the news hoping it takes my mind off hunger. My eyes pop open when the door swings wide. I fell asleep even after all the hours in the car.

The smell of pizza hits my nose. Rack has a large pizza box in one hand, some bags swinging under it, a six pack of water, and another bag in the other hand. I need clothes, but eating is definitely first on the list.

"Drop the food right here on the bed, buster, and I'll try to leave you a slice." I pull the sheet up with me when I sit because I know the shirt I'm wearing has ridden up and the poor man doesn't need to see my overly large belly. I glance up after arranging myself and he's grinning at me. God, the dimples will seriously do me in. A grin changes his face to a whole new level of attractive. Add the scruff on his jaw and killer lips and I'm having heart palpitations.

I smile back when he places the bags and pizza box on the bed. I tear open the lid and inhale. I rip out a piece and start chowing down. Rack tosses me some napkins, but I'm too interested in filling my mouth with pizza to care if I make a mess. I groan as I chew the first bite. Heaven. I hate Angelo all over again. A girl must have junk food now and then, and a pregnant woman should have anything her body craves.

Rack sits on the other side of the bed and I nudge the box in his direction without taking time away from stuffing my face. I receive his dimpled smile again. He's much more civilized about the food and takes his sweet time removing a slice from the box.

I swallow my fourth bite and wipe my mouth. "Can I have your babies and darn your socks for the rest of my life?" It's a joke and the last thing I expect is for his smile to disappear.

"Sure," he whispers.

The atmosphere changes and the room grows smaller, or at least feels that way. I think he's serious. Then again, I'm a horrible judge of men and this is nothing but wishful thinking on my part. No, I don't want to kiss him and if I say it in my head a million times it might be true.

I toss out humor to keep my sanity. "I know you've left trampled hearts behind. Tell me about the special girl waiting for you in Arizona."

His expression remains indifferent and he shakes his head. "No one waiting. You're the only special girl I know."

Pregnancy brain is making me read things into his words that aren't there. I place the half-eaten piece of pizza back in the box and give a nervous giggle. "Just me—the pregnant woman who messed up her life so bad a madman wants her dead as soon as his baby is born? If you think that's special, you need psychiatric help." I keep my voice light and teasing.

He studies me and then replies, "There's dessert, so eat your pizza."

I look at the other bags on the bed. "You brought dessert?"

"You don't get to peek until you're finished eating," he teases and graces me with another smile.

I pick up the discarded slice and finish it in three very unladylike bites. I reach for another and then freeze. Angelo trained me too well and I'm expecting a slap on my hand or face. The light mood of a moment before crumbles and I glance up at Rack in fear.

A lethal glare replaces his gentle look and I snap my hand back with guilt. Rack moves slowly and pushes the box in my direction. I inhale and more guilt weighs me down. This is not Angelo. Rack is a good guy and I have no reason to be afraid of him. "Habit, sorry," I mumble.

Rack stands and walks around the bed until he's beside me. He cups my face in his palms, tilting my head in his direction. "Don't ever be sorry," he says in a rough voice. "Angelo will never lay a hand on you again. Now eat and you can have all the dessert."

I truly do want to have his babies. It doesn't matter that I'm delusional. Rack is the perfect man and I would give anything to be the woman who rocks his world. He releases me and my fuzzy Rack-induced brain clears. I take a third piece of pizza after he moves away. He picks up three of the four plastic bags and tosses them on the other bed. At his movement, I notice a dark spot sticking to his skin on the right side of his T-shirt. It looks like blood. Was he hurt rescuing me?

"Rack," I say drawing out the one syllable. He glances over. "What's wrong with your side?"

He lifts his arm and peers down and then shrugs. "It's a scrape, nothing to worry about." He glances at the television without meeting my eyes.

I put my pizza slice back in the box, wipe my fingers, and do my best to push down the shirt I'm wearing beneath the sheet. I stand up and take a step toward him. "It's not a scrape. You're bleeding. You expect honesty from me and that goes both ways." A tightening of his jaw is my answer. "Let me see. Right. Now," I add like a Catholic nun standing over a misbehaving student.

Rack shakes his head. "No, Beth. I'll shower and put some antiseptic on it. It's nothing for you to worry about."

My fingers go to the hem of his T-shirt. He watches when I lift it slightly away from his side before moving it up. He has stitches. They start just above his hip. I count them; the T-shirt is stuck to his side at the ninth stitch. The edges of the wound are puffy and red. He should be in bed and not battling my demons.

"It's nothing, Beth," he grinds out.

I'm not afraid of him. Not when he's hurt and worse off because of me. "That's crap. This is not *nothing*. Did you leave the hospital to come rescue me?" I can't hide my exasperation.

He takes hold of my hands and moves them away from his chest. "No, I wasn't in the hospital. It happened in Mexico and a friend sewed me up." He releases me and steps back. "Eat. I'll take a shower and be as good as new."

I actually stomp my foot in frustration. "You won't. You can't shower with those stitches." I really want to bust him upside the head. "Take off your shirt and let me wash your side. I won't eat the pizza or have dessert unless you cooperate. Did my brother mention how stubborn I am?" My hands go to my non-existent waist.

A low rumble of laughter escapes him. "Nick did mention that once or twice. I'll sit in the chair while you eat. Then you can play doctor."

Why do those words sound so damn sexy? "Deal," I say as I sit back on the bed and finish eating. Rack takes another piece too and everything is back to normal or as normal as it can be with a pregnant woman with raging sex hormones and a semi-sex god in the same room.

The dessert bag holds two donuts with icing. "Sorry," he says. "I know I promised ice cream but shopping for your clothes took longer than I thought it would and the donut place was on the way back."

Like I care. The donuts are filled with sugar and I've craved it for too long to quibble over the type of sweet treat he brought me. I offer him the other donut and he shakes his head. I guess you don't get his body by eating donuts. I, on the other hand, have no problem eating both of them.

When I'm finished, I lick my fingers until I notice Rack watching. What can I say? They were too damn good to miss the small bits of icing on my fingers.

I lean back against the pillows and sigh. I'm ready to explode. Maybe pizza wasn't the greatest idea. I stand up carefully because of the darned shirt, tidy up the bed, and then carry the pizza box with four slices left over to the table.

"You ready?" I say over my shoulder as I walk toward the bathroom trying to ignore the stuffed feeling in my stomach.

Rack stands up. For his size he has the grace of a panther, and watching him walk is elegance in motion. He picks up the handgun he gave me earlier and brings it into the bathroom with us. He's so confident and so much like my brother it hurts. Sadness rolls through me. I dig my fingernails into my palms to shake away the pain. I remove the items I need from Rack's kit, which holds first aid supplies as well as bathroom necessities.

"Are you supposed to be taking these?" I hold up a bottle labeled amoxicillin on a plain white label. There's no name for the person the pills are prescribed to, which seems strange.

"Give me two," Rack says in his deep voice that fills the small space. I open the bottle and hand over two large pills. He pops them in his mouth and swallows without water. Such a macho man. I hide a smile and turn on the tap.

When the water is warm, I wet a washcloth. "We need to soak the blood so the shirt doesn't stick to your side. It's tricky because you really shouldn't get stitches wet."

"No need," Rack says and before I can stop him, he whips the shirt over his head.

I'd move back if there was space. Holy shit he's big and his bare chest makes him appear more so. I'm once again fascinated by his tattoos. They're obviously religious. I'll ask him another time. Right now my eyes turn to the problem at hand.

Ignore his muscles, ignore his muscles, I recite silently.

The blood trailing down his side makes me forget his sexy torso for a moment. I suddenly want to throttle him for pulling the shirt off with no thought to his injury. "Stop with the tough act," I snap. "You're doing more harm than good. Now turn and let me get to work, you idiot."

Yep, I just called the man who saved me an idiot. It was that or place my hand on my chest to slow my heart palpitations. No man should look this good. No man should smell this good after wearing the same clothes overnight. No musky cologne odor either. Angelo used too much and in the first few months of my pregnancy I was nauseous every time he came near. Rack smells like a real man, which sounds stupid. I can't help it, though. His scent kicks my hormones into overdrive.

He steps closer, turns, and lifts his arm. The wound extends upward from his hip and ends under his arm. "How did you manage this?" I ask while dabbing the washcloth on the dried blood at the top of the injury.

"Knife," he grunts.

Not what I expected. On-the-job injury or something. Not a knife. "Where did it happen?"

"Mexico."

That most likely explains the prescription label. I have a sneaking suspicion he's some kind of mercenary. I picture him hiring out to foreign governments in need of top-notch ex-soldiers to save the citizens from tyranny. I can totally romanticize him working for the better good of humankind.

He stands still as I clean him from pit to hip. The wound is deeper in the middle where it bled so much and stuck to his shirt. "I'm sure push-ups aren't helping you heal," I say while rinsing out the bloody cloth for the second time.

"Needed 'em," is his clipped response.

"You need a brain transplant is what you need. This will never heal if you continue abusing yourself. I'm sorry that rescuing me is a part of the problem. You should be in bed."

I'm startled when he turns, lifts his hand, and cups my chin. He's so close—his eyes dark pools of an ignitable substance. "I will always rescue you, Beth."

My heart skips a beat. "What if I don't need rescuing?" I whisper.

His grunt is a half-laugh. "I have a feeling you'll always need rescuing."

I can't peel my gaze from his. "I'm changing my ways and taking the safe road from here on out. If you haven't noticed, I'm going to be a mother."

Rack's gaze slowly travels down to my belly and back up. "The baby will only get you in more trouble." He dips his head and his mouth is only a millimeter from mine.

My blood sizzles. "That's not nice," I answer breathlessly.

"No," his full lips brush mine. "This isn't nice."

He kisses me—puts his lips over mine and makes me gasp into his mouth. He slips his tongue inside without hesitation. His taste and mastery consume me. I'm no virgin to kissing but God, never like this. He adds gentle pressure to my chin and angles my head slightly to the right. The kiss turns from sensual to devouring. I'm completely lost in the touch of our lips and tongues. He grabs my ass with his free hand and hauls me against his body.

Is this kiss nice? Hell no. It's deep and dirty. How can he do this with just his mouth? I need oxygen and I don't think I've taken a breath since the kiss began. He pulls back enough to bite at my lips and run his tongue across the places he nips. My eyes are closed but now I open them slowly and come back to the real world. In a bathroom. Rack's shirt off. His hand on my ass. My very fat belly pressed against him. God. His erection pressing into me.

"That shouldn't have happened," he groans without releasing me or moving his lips away.

"No, but will you do it again?" I sigh. I don't care if I sound like I'm begging. I am.

He smiles with the full dimpled grin I love. His hand leaves my chin and skims down my neck and around my shoulder so his fingers splay across my back. His mouth and tongue take over and everything wrong in my life recedes to the background. I feel like a woman for the first time in months. I move my hands to his hips half on his cargo pants and half on bare skin.

This man has turned me into an inferno of need.

I. Want.

Chapter Thirteen

Rack

I've never deviated from a mission or allowed anyone to sway me from my goals. This woman is different. She's trouble. It must be all the stories her brother spilled. I remember Nick telling me each escapade in hilarious detail. When she was nine she grabbed a woman's leg in a convenience store who was shoplifting and refused to let go. She yelled, "Thief, thief," until the entire shopping public came to see what was happening. When a few years older she stepped in front of a man who was threatening to hit his wife. Nick said she saw no gray in the world and lived for justice. She has the same ethics as my family—good people with a defined line between right and wrong. I can't have her. She'd never survive my life. Even though she says she'll kill Angelo, she wouldn't. Her moral compass is set in stone.

I break the kiss that I should never have started. She's breathless, her mouth wet from my lips. She's so damn sexy...and soft...and desirable. Her flushed cheeks, filled out by the pregnancy, make her more womanly than she appeared the first time I met her. It kills me to back away. I want to show her how sexy she is, how turned on I am. Hell, I don't even know if she can have sex safely. I like it rough and dirty, so to answer my own silent questions: It's a hell no. And as quick as the thought enters my mind another takes over. For her I could be gentle and fuck her nice and slow. My dick is talking to my brain and my brain is saying hell yes. Unfortunately, I'm the worst thing that could ever happen to her.

"I'm so fat," she says when my grip loosens and she realizes the moment is over.

That's not what I want to hear from her. I want her to feel desirable even if I can't have her. "Yeah, so?" I breathe against her mouth.

Her smile knocks me sideways. "You're supposed to disagree."

"Have you looked in the mirror?"

She pinches my uninjured side. "I like that you don't lie to me."

Her words pull me from the spell we're in. She has no idea who I really am. The thought of seeing her hero worship dim when she discovers the truth hurts. "I have more lies buried than you could ever imagine." I release her and take her small hands off my waist. One of us needs to be strong. "I'll finish up. I'm taking a shower whether you approve or not."

Her gaze turns hard. "No shower."

My hand moves to my swollen cock and her eyes follow. "I need...a shower."

"Oh," she whispers, her expressive eyes going wide. "I um, could um..." Her cheeks flush even more.

I picture her on her knees and my cock down her throat. I hold back a groan. "No, you can't," I say sternly and leave no room for misunderstanding. She's killing me. She steps back and the uncertainty in her expression guts me.

I close the bathroom door and swear softly into the room so she doesn't hear me. She has absolutely no idea how sexy she is—swollen belly and all. I turn on the shower and shuck my pants and boxers. I should use cold water to get myself under control. It won't work. I soap myself up and picture Beth on her knees, her mouth around my cock, eyes peering up at me caught somewhere between innocence and vixen. Fuck but I want her. Telling myself she's pregnant with another man's child does nothing to stop the need igniting in my cock. I want to sink into her heat and get lost.

I'm fucking everything up.

I groan loudly when I come against the shower wall. I'm beyond worrying if she hears. This is what she's done to me. When the last drop of cum slides down the shower drain, I gingerly wash my side and then my body. Before leaving the shower, I rub another one out. I've got to sleep in the bed across from her all night and this is the only way I'll survive.

With a towel around my hips, I leave the bathroom. Beth is asleep. The covers are pushed down and there's a pillow propped between her legs. Christ, she slays me. As I gaze at her, unable to look away, I realize her back must hurt from carrying the extra weight. She hasn't complained. She's like her brother in that. Things could be fuck-all bad and Nick could make everyone around him laugh.

I need to control myself and focus on the problem at hand. Beth is in danger and that's where my thoughts should be. I move three handguns to the corner table and pull out a small cleaning kit. When I need to think, the best way to do it is to clean my weapons. I remove the first magazine, expel the round from the chamber, and dismantle the gun. I open the cleaning solvent and breathe in deeply, allowing the smell to put me in the proper head space.

I need a plan. In her condition, taking her to Mexico and leaving her in a safe house is out of the question. She needs good quality medical care and that alone is tricky. I don't have the connections Moon and Gomez do, and I can't obtain a fake ID without their help. We can ditch the Jeep and I can pick up something cheap that Angelo can't track as easily. That will be step one.

I push a cloth patch through the barrel and then wipe it down with the rag. I don't even think about what I'm doing, it's muscle memory. My life and Beth's depend on having weapons that work.

To get her out of the country, somewhere safer than Mexico, she'll need a passport. Again, not something I can do without help. To be on the safe side, I need to factor in the child's birth. That gives me two weeks to set her up near a medical facility. We need cash. I have a few thousand on me but it's not enough. I have slightly over thirty grand in an American bank. Taking out money from my account will tip off Angelo, but I don't think we can help it.

I wipe cleaning solvent and oil off my hands and use my phone to search craigslist for a vehicle. I see a few possibilities. After reassembling the Glock, I move to the next handgun. It's dark outside by the time I'm finished.

A small moan escapes Beth and she rolls over so she's facing me. Her eyes slowly open and she blinks a few times. Her soft sleepy eyes are sexy and I'm heading back to the territory I need to avoid. She moves her head and glances at the bedside clock. "I can't believe how much I'm sleeping," she says groggily before getting up and heading into the bathroom. She sticks her head out a minute later. "Any chance you bought me something to sleep in?"

It never occurred to me, and I shake my head. "I have another T-shirt you can use. I did buy you a toothbrush and deodorant."

She smiles, walks over to the bags on my bed, sits down, and opens them. I had to guess on sizes and figured too small wouldn't cut it, so I went a size larger than I thought she might need. She pulls out a pair of those half pant half short things women wear and laughs again. She stands up and slips them on. They have the pregnant belly elastic at the top. They're big on her and she laughs some more.

"Sorry about that, I didn't want to get them too small."

"They're great. Angelo wanted me in tight clothing even though they were uncomfortable."

I add another reason to kill the twat.

"These are baggy but they'll stay up." She pulls one of the shirts out of a bag and heads back into the bathroom. She comes out wearing a pink stretch top that shows off her round belly. My eyes travel down to her bare toes. She wiggles them. "My feet are swollen and I don't think I can get back into my shoes right now."

I also didn't think to buy shoes. "We aren't going anywhere until morning. Do you have a problem with more pizza for dinner?"

She looks at the box and I would swear she turns a little green.

"I can go out and get us something. You name it and it's yours."

She shakes her head. "No, it's all good. I'm not actually hungry. I haven't eaten so much since before I met Angelo."

She's giving me the perfect lead-in. "Why don't you sit down and tell me how you got involved with Angelo Gimonde."

She gives me sad puppy dog eyes but it won't work. "Just saying I was stupid won't cut it?"

I shake my head and use my foot to push out the chair across from me. I place the cleaning items away, reload the last gun, and look expectantly at Beth.

"Fine," she says like a child, which is actually pretty damn cute. She takes a minute to rub her lower back before sitting down and placing her elbows on the table. She rests her chin in her hands. "You remember Kevin?"

With her brother cussing out the man from day one and meeting the worm in person the first time I met Beth, I doubt I'll ever forget him. "Yes," I grunt.

"I should have listened to my brother. Kevin is a certified turd." She stands up, walks over to the bottles of water on the floor next to her bed, and removes two from the plastic securing them. She hands me one and then takes a seat again. "You didn't meet Sheila. She was my bestie from college. I don't have a lot of friends, and I asked her to be my maid of honor." Beth's expression turns hard even though she's doing her best to keep the conversation light. "She flew in from New York the day before the wedding. The third and final date of our wedding. When I met you, it was right before the first date we set." She looks around the room for a minute before continuing. "Kevin took us out to dinner so he could get to know her. He couldn't take his eyes off her. That's a normal reaction from men when it comes to Sheila, so I didn't think much of it. We did a little dancing and I still didn't connect the dots when they danced a few slow songs and talked the entire time." She takes a drink and gathers herself. I know exactly where this is going and I'm gritting my teeth. "Kevin dropped us at my apartment and we went upstairs to have a girl's all-night talking marathon before the wedding. Around two in the morning, Sheila received a text message and asked if I would be hurt if she met up with a hot guy she met at the dance club. What could I say?" Beth sucks in a long steady breath. "I'm not stupid. I laid in bed and put two and two together. I hoped I was being paranoid the entire time I drove to Kevin's place. I had a key and let myself in." She gazes down at her clenched hands. "My best friend and my fiancé were doing the dirty on the living room floor. They couldn't even wait to get to the bed." She wipes tears from her eyes and I would strangle the fucktard if he were here right now.

"He's a twat," I state emphatically.

I receive a soft smile. "Thank you."

"For what?"

She shrugs. "For not offering me your pity. He is a twat and I'm glad I didn't marry him. The only problem was the giant hole in my heart. Angelo stepped in at just the right time and filled it. He wined and dined me. Said he was a businessman taking a break from the real world. My heart was ripped to shreds, and, like an idiot, I fell for every line of crap Angelo gave me. My brother would have seen through Angelo immediately. Hell, a child could have seen through him." The tears flow faster and I push my chair out so I can stand up and pull her against my chest. I freeze when she places her hand toward me palm out. "Let me finish. I never cried this much before I got pregnant and admitting my stupidity isn't fun." She sniffs and continues after I sit down again. "Angelo was perfect in every way. Too perfect. He gave me expensive jewelry. He told me the world was our playground and he wanted me by his side." She shakes her head subtly at the memories. "He had bodyguards and I never questioned why. He wasn't a celebrity but I had stars in my eyes. Someone rich and successful wanted me. By the time I realized things were not as they seemed, I discovered I was pregnant. I told Angelo and he was ecstatic. He planned for me to meet his family. The niggling doubts remained, but I was going to meet his family in Chicago and we would announce our engagement and follow that with a quick wedding. He wouldn't listen to my reservations. I don't know why I didn't check into him in the beginning. I only did it after overhearing his bodyguards discussing me and how the baby would put Angelo back in his father's good graces. My Internet search told me enough that I knew I could never marry him." She lifts trembling fingers to her cheeks. "That was the first time Angelo hit me. He forced me into his car and took me to his house."

I'm too angry to sit, but I know this is hard for her so I stand slowly and do my best to keep my voice even. "How did you contact me?"

"The man you shot at the front door, Peter. He left his phone in his room and I saw it when I tried to find a jacket so I could walk outside."

"Did you care about Peter?" It doesn't really matter. I had no choice. I just want to know if it bothers her.

Beth gives me a shaky smile. "He was just a kid with hero worship. Angelo would have killed him if he knew I sent the message from Peter's phone. I knew that and sent a message anyway."

In this, she's exactly like her brother—do what needs doing even if you don't like it. She has Nick's dark eyes. He was so damn proud of Beth in everything but her choice of men. Of course he thought I was the better choice. More fool him.

The words slip out before I can stop them. "Do you want a back rub?"

Chapter Fourteen

To: Beth Hoffman,
Enclosed you will find your brother's final communication. He has paid the ultimate sacrifice to his country and so has his family. I grieve with you.
Commander E. Montgomery

Dearest Beth,
By now you know I didn't keep my promise and that I'm not coming home. Forgive me. I would give anything to see you grow into a more incredible woman, find that special man who completes you, and make baby Beths who will be as cute as you. From the moment you were born, I loved you. I hear that's rather strange for older brothers but to me you were the perfect bundle of joy and you gave my life purpose. This is actually the second "just in case" letter I've written. This new one is because of my friendship with Rack. I've beat you upside the head about him. I won't do it in this letter. But I need you to know that he will always be there for you. You can depend on him no matter the circumstances. Grieve for me and then move on with your life. I want your happiness above all else. I will love you until the end of time and beyond.
Your everything brother,
Nick

* * * *

Beth

Rack just asked if I want a pot of gold. It's sad that the hardest thing about being under Angelo's proverbial thumb was the lack of touch. The baby hormones only made it worse. My back aches constantly, along with my feet and calves. I wake up with calf cramps that leave me in tears.

"Please," I whisper, afraid he'll take back the offer.

His dimples appear and he waves his hand toward the bed. "I can't get to your lower back while you're in the chair."

I jump up and head to the bathroom. "I'm putting your shirt back on," I say over my shoulder. He's going to touch me again. I tear my clothes off and pull his T-shirt over my head. My panties, hanging over the curtain rod, are almost dry, so I slip them on. I walk out and Rack is standing next to the bed where he's pulled back the covers. "If I lay face down, I'll need multiple pillows above and below my belly. Can you toss over some from your bed?"

Rack hands me two pillows from his bed and I add them to my two. I make two piles with enough room for my belly to rest between them. As I look at what I'm about to do, I realize I'll look like a beached whale once I'm lying down. I back away. "I've changed my mind. I don't feel like a back rub right now."

He looks at the bed and then at me. "What's wrong? I thought you wanted a back massage."

He's so perfect. So beautiful. So damn hot. "I'm fat," I say in frustration. I point at my ass. "Do you know what this will look like propped up by pillows?"

The jerk smiles. "I thought we already established that you're fat. Baby fat."

I want to laugh, yell, and stomp my feet at the same time. "Sometimes it might work in your favor to lie to a girl."

His expression changes and he appears more closed off. I've said the wrong thing. Then his gaze lightens and he places his hand out. I slowly lift mine and take his fingers. "I promise this will feel great," he says huskily.

The blood in my veins catches fire. I'm practically breathless. Too many thoughts fly through my head. Could this turn into sex? Would he want it to? Will my expanded body repulse him?

He reads something in my gaze. "Only a back rub." He pulls me closer to the bed and I turn slightly and look up at him. I'm disappointed but I understand. I'm an idiot for thinking this sexy man could want me.

"Turn around so I can situate myself," I tell him before I chicken out and end the chance of him touching me.

He chuckles, shakes his head, and turns like I asked. I climb onto the bed, pull the T-shirt down, and do my best to position the pillows beneath my hips and breasts. "Okay," I say with a huff from the exertion. "Make it good because I don't know if I'll ever have the guts to do this again." I gaze down at the sheet and refuse to watch Rack when he gets his first look at me.

He doesn't say anything, thank God. His knee dips into the mattress and he shifts closer. One leg goes over me so he's straddling my upper thighs. I'm about to call a halt to everything because I'm mortified by how I must look to a man who most likely has gorgeous women in his bed whenever he's in the mood. I say nothing because his fingers span my lower back and dig in just enough to bring a moan from deep in my throat.

"Is that okay?" he asks as his hands massage upward.

"Oh, God, yes. Don't stop." I'm in heaven. Tingles follow everywhere he touches. I can't stop the noises that rise from my throat. His large hands move up and down my back, over my shoulders and finally he moves lower to my ass. I don't have the willpower to stop him. He kneads the muscles, and the moan I'm in the middle of turns to a loud embarrassing groan. This isn't sex, but maybe it's better. I hadn't realized how bad my muscles needed this attention.

"What about your thighs and calves?" he asks.

"Yes, please," I say with a heavy breath because nothing has ever felt this good in my entire life.

He moves to my thighs, shifts his body so he's beside me, and rubs farther down my legs. He massages my feet without asking. Why hasn't some woman snatched him up? I would have ten babies and never complain if a man would do this each time I was pregnant.

His hands drift back up and my eyelids grow heavy. He lightly trails his hands over my skin; the rough callouses on his fingers adding to the sensation. His hands still and I roll over to my back. He moves the pillows away so I'm comfortable. His eyes are jade green—dark and dreamy, full of need. I tear my gaze away and look lower. God, his erection. I want to see him naked. I want to wrap my mouth around him and give him the best blow job of his life.

"I need another shower," he says softly, and I look back into his eyes.

"You do because I just had at least five orgasms," I say with a smile. It's the first time he gives me a full out laugh. He's even more beautiful. "Will you kiss me again, Rack?" I ask when his laughter fades.

"No."

"Lie to me," I beg.

"I'll never lie to you, Beth. You have questions, you ask."

I reach out and take his hand, placing it on my breast. His fingers squeeze gently. My breasts are extra sensitive and I inhale sharply. "Don't stop," I whisper. I feel like he doesn't want this to happen and I almost roll away.

He bends down and kisses me. My fingers go to his head and weave into his hair. It's longer now than it was when I first met him and it's so darn soft. My desire fires on all cylinders. He moves the pillows further away and ends the kiss, just looking at me for a few seconds. Before I beg, his hand slips inside the shirt and his rough fingers slide over my nipple. I arch into him, almost forgetting that I'm pregnant. His face is so intent on what he's doing. He watches me—my face, my expression. His eyes are murky with desire. His other hand travels to the bottom of the shirt and slides under it as he leans over me. His fingers travel across my thigh and when he encounters my panties, he slips past them. I'm wet. I want him. A single finger enters me and I close my eyes and press my pelvis into his touch.

"Oh, God." My breath comes in gasps. Rack's musky scent fills me. My heart pounds and my blood heats. He kisses me again. His lips are so perfect, so commanding. He turns my entire world upside down, consuming me. His tongue dances to the same rhythm as his finger. I cry out when he slips two fingers inside. He immediately stops and begins pulling his hand away. I grab his arm. "No, no, don't stop. Please don't stop." I croon into his mouth. I'm desperate. His touch is all-consuming. I can't stop myself from grinding against his hand...wanting more, needing everything he's willing to give.

His fingers slip away and I want to scream. Then he brings them up and slides them over my mouth, painting my lips with my own wetness. His smoky, green, lust-filled eyes follow his fingers—so intent on the artistry. When my lips are wet, I lick just the bottom one and taste. His eyes go from steamy to hot emerald. He lowers his lips and his nostrils flair as he inhales. His tongue comes out and runs over where I just licked. Then, he glides it across my upper lip and makes a noise deep in his throat. His mouth claims mine, so I swallow his groan and it combines with my own. His fingers trail downward over the T-shirt and I don't care about my fat belly, I want his touch on bare flesh.

His fingers sink inside me again. Slowly in and just as slowly out. The rough pad of his thumb circles my clit. The air in the room no longer holds enough oxygen. I push up against his hand when his two fingers sink deep. He increases the rhythm—driving me insane with need. The spasms start too soon. I want this to last forever, but my body has other ideas. Rack is no longer kissing me. He's watching me. I shake my head back and forth.

"Let go, Beth," he commands.

"You..." I fight my body. "You don't understand," I manage to strangle out before the internal pulses explode and I can't think. Oh, but I feel. It's earth shattering. The aftershocks come one after the other until I'm completely undone.

I recover slowly and I'm suddenly aware of Rack's erection pressing against my side. My right hand is trapped between our bodies, so I turn slightly to my side and run my left hand down his chest to reach for his cock. His hand takes mine, lifts it, and kisses the backs of my fingers. He pulls away and slowly rises off the bed. I want to scream. He kisses my nose and without another word, disappears into the bathroom. I should feel ashamed that I was such a wanting mess of need. Later, maybe. Right now I sink into the sensation of having the best orgasm of my life. It doesn't matter that he left me because I still feel his touch and it goes clear to my soul.

The miserable sexual ache I've carried for so long is gone. I smooth my palm over my tummy. The baby is a tight, hard ball beneath the stretched skin.

"I think I'm a little in love with him," I whisper into the room after the shower goes on.

I fall asleep with a smile on my lips.

Chapter Fifteen

Rack

I jack off three times before I'm willing to even think about returning to the bedroom. She is so incredibly soft, her pussy so fucking hot. And, God, her taste. I'll never get it out of my head. The remembrance of her sweet scent mixes up my insides until I'm one raging hard-on after another. How the hell will I walk away once she's safe?

The hero worship shows plainly in her eyes. She thinks I'm a man like her brother and has no idea who and what I really am—a cold-blooded killer with a vendetta that eats him alive. Beth deserves something more. She deserves a man without blood on his hands. I rest my forehead against the shower wall. What the hell am I doing? It doesn't matter that watching her come was the sexiest thing I've ever seen.

I fucked this up royally.

I'm relieved when I enter the bedroom and she's asleep. I want to leave early tomorrow morning, so I place all but one handgun in the weapons bag, tidy the room, and hit the bed wearing boxers. It doesn't take much for me to fall asleep. It's been a long few days.

Beth gets up twice during the night to use the bathroom. I'm instantly back to sleep when she climbs back into her bed.

* * * *

I check my phone for messages before the sun comes up. There's another text from Gomez.

Check your old email

I stare at the message for several minutes. I only have one email account, which is on my phone, and there are no messages waiting. And it's strange that he would use it anyway. It suddenly dawns on me that I do have another email address. It's the one from my other life. It's been a long time since I checked it and I've never used my phone or the laptop in my room at Moon's compound when I did. The fact Gomez sent a message to my old email means things are hot on his end.

I can't worry about that right now. Beth and I need a safe place to hunker down until the baby's born. There are several possibilities. Today, we'll get enough cash to enable us to do what's needed, including the car issue.

With the lights out, I look through the front window into the parking lot. As long as the Jeep's license plate didn't hit any cameras, Angelo will think I'm heading in Moon's direction. Staying a state over won't keep us safe for long, though.

I quietly carry the bags out to the Jeep before waking Beth. The light is just beginning to shine through the curtains when I gently nudge her shoulder.

"Wanna sleep," she sluggishly whispers. Her hair is tousled and she's more beautiful than ever.

I steel myself against giving in and letting her sleep. She can nap on the road. "No can do. We have a long day ahead of us and I know you must be starving."

"Eat pizza," she says and pulls a pillow over her head.

I remove the pillow and slide my hand under the sheet. My plan is to tickle her. Or that was the plan. My hand slides over her stomach and I feel a strong kick under my palm. "Shit," I say and jerk my hand back.

"Oh gosh, you can't make a pregnant woman laugh before she pees first thing in the morning. Those are the rules," she says with a laugh that turns into a groan.

I'm smiling when I whip back the covers to help her out of bed. Her fingers scramble to pull my shirt over her belly. I place my hand over both of hers. "Now that I know there's not an alien under there can I feel the baby kick again?"

"I really need to pee," she answers as she takes my hand and moves it farther up her stomach. Thirty seconds later I feel another kick. I'm watching her stomach and see movement. "She's rolling over," Beth adds with a soft smile when I look back into her eyes.

"Damn. Does it hurt?"

She laughs again. "The only thing that hurts right now is my bladder. Help me up, please."

I hear her desperation. I lift her from the bed and stand her next to it. She wobbles for a few seconds and then turns and heads into the bathroom. Thirty minutes later, we pull into a drive-thru for breakfast. Beth orders two breakfast croissants, hash browns, and two milks. I don't say a word.

I give her an overview of what today's plans are. "We're hitting the bank as soon as it opens and then buying a car. I have two promising leads. Taking money from the bank will give Gimonde our location. We'll leave quickly and drive to the location of the first car, hoping we get lucky. I picked up a throwaway phone when I shopped yesterday. Mine will stay behind after we go to the bank. If they're able to track it, we might as well give them someplace they would find anyway. Once we're in a different vehicle, we'll use the new phone and we'll be untraceable."

I explain it all while driving west. "The vehicles I checked on and got addresses for are in Moab, Utah. It's a small town but has a direct route into Arizona. That's where Gimonde will think we're heading. After we have the new vehicle, we'll head east." Beth doesn't argue. "You feeling okay?" I finally ask.

"Ate too much again. If you see a donut shop on the way, don't pass it by, though."

She's killing me and I want to stop the car and kiss her again. "Deal," I say instead.

We take several bathroom breaks, eat lunch, and arrive in Moab around two in the afternoon. One of the reasons I chose this location was because my bank is one of three in town. I pull out all but a grand so I don't need to waste time closing the account. Because I'm withdrawing a large amount, an assistant manager comes over and helps with the transaction.

"Would you like your balance, Mr. Jones?" the teller asks right before I turn away.

"Yes, please." She hands me the slip and I walk out. We're on the clock now and need to move quickly. Beth waits in the Jeep with one of the guns in her lap. I hand her the receipt and pouch with the money.

"We're heading to the first vehicle I found for sale." I notice her looking down at the receipt.

"What do you actually do for a living?" she asks.

I knew the question would come up eventually. "I work security for Xavier Moon." If she recognizes his name, my answer will lead to more questions. I told her I wouldn't lie. There are things I can't talk about and I'll relay exactly that if her questions touch sensitive areas.

She looks back down at the receipt. "He must pay quite well."

I think about my foreign account with more than ten times what this one has. "Moon takes care of his employees," is all I say.

"I've never seen half a million dollars even on paper."

"What?"

"You withdrew thirty thousand dollars and have half a million left. I can't even imagine."

I place my hand out and she hands me the receipt. I'm driving, so I take only a quick look at the small paper. Sure enough, I have five hundred and one thousand dollars remaining.

"Gomez," I mutter.

"Is that code for something?"

"He's a friend who also works for Moon. It's his way of helping us."

"With a half million dollars?" she asks, shocked.

"Yes." My brain is stumbling over the reality that Moon and Gomez are refusing to back down on this. I turn down a residential road and find the house I'm looking for. Before we look at the vehicle, I check my old email and sure enough, Gomez tells me he's put money in my account.

The vehicle we came to see has a for sale sign in the back window. "We're married," I tell Beth. "Let me do the talking." A funny look appears on her face but she doesn't argue. I emailed this guy earlier and he's expecting us. The garage door rolls up and he walks out. Beth and I get out of the Jeep and I walk around and take her hand. I let her go when I shake Charlie's hand.

He's somewhere in his sixties with a beer belly that says he enjoys food and drink a little too much. He smiles at Beth when he notices her stomach and I decide he's a nice guy.

"We're looking for a second vehicle for my wife to drive short distances after the baby's born," I tell him. He walks us through everything about the car—an older white Honda Civic with low miles. It's a one-owner vehicle and in great condition for its age. Charlie jumps in the back and we take her for a test drive. I ask Beth her opinion on the way back to Charlie's.

"You know I don't know anything about cars, sweetie. I'll leave this decision in your hands."

She's such a smartass, just like Nick said. We head to Charlie's bank so he can notarize the title after I dicker over the price a bit and hand six grand over. From start to finish, we buy the car in less than an hour and drive away. Beth follows in the Jeep. I head to the small Moab airport twelve miles away. Beth parks a mile from the airport and we transfer everything into the new car. When we're done, she waits for me to ditch the Jeep in the parking lot. Moab airport has a small commercial service that flies to Salt Lake City and Denver. The Jeep won't become a problem with airport personnel for a week or two. I toss my personal cell phone into some roadside bushes on the way back to Beth. We're heading to Colorado through back roads and it will take two hours longer. Beth has her seat fully reclined by the time we hit the Colorado border. She moves around a lot to get comfortable but doesn't complain other than to ask for frequent bathroom breaks.

Neither of us mentions what happened last night. It's better this way.

I bypass Denver and take another back road to Colorado Springs, where I jump on Route 24 that intersects with I-70. At least the weather is warmer here. Colorado Springs reminds me of Phoenix with a little more green and a slightly milder temperature. Beth says she's not hungry, so we leave the city without eating, though I grab a couple of water bottles out of the back.

"Damn, damn, damn," Beth whispers an hour outside of Colorado Springs.

"You okay?"

She buries her face in her hands and doesn't look at me when she whispers, "My water broke."

"Here," I hand mine in her direction. "There's more in the back." I glance at her when she doesn't take it.

Her eyes are huge. "Not that water. The baby's water."

It takes a few seconds for her words to register. With calm I don't feel, I put on the blinker and pull off the highway before coming to a stop. A million things run through my head. I take Beth's shaking hand. "I know very little about childbirth." That's a damned understatement. "How long do you think you have?"

She shakes her hand. "I don't know. My back's been cramping for hours. I thought it was from staying in the same position." Her other hand presses against her stomach. "First babies usually take longer but I really don't know." Her voice quivers on the last words.

"Colorado Springs will have a hospital. We'll be there in forty-five minutes." My plan is to drive like a bat out of hell.

Her gaze doesn't leave mine. A tear rolls down her cheeks. "We can't. He'll find me there."

I'm fully aware of that. "I'll get you there and you'll contact the police immediately."

Her lips tremble even more. "He killed a man in front of me. He…he left me in the room with the body for hours." Her voice rises. "He'll kill people to get me back." Her eyes change and I see Nick's calm resolve staring at me. "No hospital."

My fury at Angelo ignites again. Keeping my voice calm isn't easy. "He won't get near you. I'll be in the wings and I promise to keep you safe." I don't tell her I'll die keeping my promise. This is Angelo's child. He'll bring his father in if he hasn't already. I'm so far over my head it's pathetic.

Involving Gomez and Moon might be my only option.

Chapter Sixteen

Beth

The brighter future for my child has just taken a nose dive. This can't be happening, but the small regular ache in my lower back and my wet maternity crop pants say differently. I can't go to a hospital. Babies are born every day in a natural environment, I reassure myself.

I lift my hand from my stomach and place it on top of Rack's. "Angelo will kill you. He'll kill anyone who gets in his way. Get us to a hotel. I'll tell you what you need to purchase. Women have been having babies by themselves since the dawn of time. I can do it." I say the words out loud because I'm terrified and actually need to reassure myself. I'd never forgive myself if something happened to the baby.

Rack looks away. I have no idea what he's thinking. The quiet in the car makes a few minutes seem like hours. He finally looks ahead, throws the car in gear, and turns around. He's taking me to the hospital. I can't stop panic from gripping me, and my heart races uncontrollably.

Rack turns my way and offers a reassuring smile. "I have an idea. To put it in play, you need to keep the baby inside you for at least five hours."

That's too ridiculous to acknowledge but it doesn't matter. I'm so relieved a flood of tears streams down my face.

"Hey," he says. "I'll deliver the baby if I need to. Stop worrying about it. I promise you'll both be safe."

I cover my face as I try to gain control. My pants are wet and uncomfortable. The seat's wet too. I'm two for two on messing up

Rack's vehicles. I take a few deep breaths and reach into the back seat where the bags of clothes are. I take out Rack's T-shirt that I wore to bed last night and place it under me. I need to time my contractions. It will give me something to do besides worry.

Once we hit the city again, he leaves me in the car and goes into a large discount store with a list of the items I hastily wrote out. It takes him thirty minutes. My contractions aren't steady. I had several at eight plus minutes and two interspersed at about three minutes. Rack finally jumps back into the car and we take off.

"Have you thought of names?" he asks after offering another reassuring smile.

He's trying to distract me and I'm thankful. "Not really. Angelo had names picked out. The last thing I'll do is use his. Maybe Gracie or Addison?"

"I like both of those," he says and then hesitates a moment. I watch his fingers gripping the steering wheel, confident in everything he does. Those large hands might deliver my baby. "What about boy names? Maybe you should have one on standby," he says and takes me out of my current thought process.

A cramp tightens my belly and I try not to grimace. Rack waits patiently for my reply. "No boys allowed," I breathe while leaning forward and rubbing my back. "If this were a boy, he would be late not early."

Rack laughs and a weight lifts off my shoulders. If he can laugh about anything right now we're doing better than I thought. My due date is closer to three weeks away than four and I know the baby is a good size. If I had to choose a competent midwife, hero, problem solver, it would be the man sitting beside me.

"Tell me about your brother. In the last email from Nick he said your brother died," I ask because I need more to think about than the current situation. When I met Rack for the first time, I never asked about his brother. I was too wrapped in my own grief combined with happiness at my coming wedding and didn't take time to delve further into Rack's life.

Rack thrums his fingers on the steering wheel. "Andrew was the baby of the family."

"If I remember right, you were one of five boys. Your poor mother." Nick loved hearing stories about Rack's family and he shared some of them with me.

Rack smiles while watching the road and his dimple shows. "There is nothing poor about my mother. That woman had a wicked right arm when holding a wooden spoon." He's quiet and I let him gather his thoughts, though I'm smiling too. "Andrew was like Nick—full of life, solid, an all-around great guy. He joined border patrol as soon as he turned eighteen. I thought he would go the military route like me, but he had his sights set on the border for some odd reason."

"Did you ever think about something else besides the military?"

"No," is his emphatic reply.

"I think that's your answer. My brother was the same way. The military appealed to him and nothing would hold him back."

We've been driving and talking for an hour when a strong contraction hits.

"So what's your big plan for this baby?"

I huff through the pain. That was a strong one.

Rack looks at the clock. "In four hours we'll reach my brother, Lincoln. He's a cop and has training in delivering babies." He doesn't give me time to soak this in. "My dad was a cop too. He delivered a baby on the side of the road a few years into his career. Made the newspapers and the parents named the baby after him.

Rack keeps talking while I watch the clock and time contractions. He tells me stories of his brothers and their escapades while growing up. We travel for two more hours. The pains are steady now and fear is making everything worse. I half-listen to Rack when he calls his brother. Two hours might be pushing it. The laugh over my silent pun turns into a groan.

Rack increases his speed.

I'm desperate. "Why did your parents name you Rack?" It fits him, but I can't imagine what the name would be like for a kid to carry around.

"It's short for Rutherford."

"Rutherford?" I ask because it seems like such a strange name.

"Rutherford Hayes Street, Andrew Jackson Street, Calvin Coolidge Street, Woodrow Wilson Street, and the brother we're heading to, Abraham Lincoln Street."

I'm breathing hard but still manage to say, "Presidents, I love it. I thought your last name was Jones?"

Chapter Seventeen

Rack

"**Now you know** my big dark secret." I laugh as a way to take her mind off the pain. She's holding tight but I don't know how long it will last. I'm terrified over delivering the baby. Give me a rifle and something to shoot—I'm your guy. Bringing a child into this world—mind numbing terror.

I thought about forgoing the call to Lincoln so he had no chance to say no. What if he wasn't there? Beth is a trouper, but I know we're almost out of time. If we're pulled over, it means we're going straight to a hospital with a police escort. I'll let fate decide. Even though my brother has training, it doesn't mean he can handle an emergency if something goes wrong.

Beth gains control and replies, "I won't tell a soul, but now I have a lot of questions. Not now, though. Can you sing?"

Her question comes out of left field. "No, not at all. You want me to turn on the radio?"

"Yeah, something mellow. I need to keep calm."

I turn on the radio. It works until we're about an hour from my brother's house.

"Turn it off," she yells and then grits her teeth and groans in pain.

I snap the music off. I start looking at highway signs. "I'll find a hotel."

"No," she groans. "Keep driving. The music hurt my ears."

I don't have a reply for that. I should be telling her to breathe or something. As far as the breathing goes she's doing well on her own. She hasn't hyperventilated. She's not screaming and she's not crying.

That changes ten minutes from our destination.

"Damn," she screams. "I can't do this. I can't."

I take the next turn on two wheels. My brother's duplex in the headlights is the best sight I've ever seen. I burn rubber coming to a stop and I'm out my door and around to Beth's side in seconds. I lift her from the car as she sobs.

"Don't let anything happen to the baby, Rack. Promise me."

I'm a few feet from the door when Linc opens it. I barrel through. "She's having a baby. I have what we need in the back seat of the car." A woman stands inside the door with a large strange-ass looking dog beside her. I don't have time for introductions because Beth screams again.

"I'll get what's in the car, Linc. Help your brother into the guest room," the woman says on her way out the door. The dog stays put with a small whine.

"What the hell are you doing, Rutherford? She needs a hospital," my brother shouts while leading the way to the back of the house.

"Yes, she does. It's not an option. She's Nick's sister and she's in trouble. I need you to deliver this baby."

The shock on Lincoln's face is comical. Not much daunts him but this has. "I can't deliver a baby," he says in horror.

"Open the damn bedroom door, I need to put her down. I'm here because they train cops to deliver babies." He steps around me, opens the door, and I carry Beth through.

"You need to put down the plastic I had you buy," Beth groans.

Fuck the plastic.

"I've got it." The woman marches past my brother with the bags from the car. She finds the plastic painter's sheet and rips it open, pulls back the bed covers, and spreads it over the bottom sheet.

"We need to call an ambulance," my brother continues arguing.

"Angelo Gimonde is the father. You've probably heard of his father who runs the Gimonde crime family. They'll kill her and take the baby."

My brother runs his hand through his hair. "Fuck, Rutherford."

"I'm Shelby by the way, your brother's next door neighbor. Lay her down on the bed. If you can't do this, Linc, go boil water or something."

If I wasn't so worried about Beth, I'd take more time to enjoy the new look on Linc's face. "You know how to deliver a baby?" he asks Shelby.

I place Beth on the bed and she grips my hand. I don't like the panicked look in her eyes. I've seen this look when soldiers are dying.

"No, but women have been doing this forever. If the two of you can't stop arguing, get out and let the ladies handle it."

"Fuck," my brother says again.

Shelby takes over and pushes pillows behind Beth's head. "No worries, you'll be fine, sweetie, and so will the baby. Linc, water. Rutherford, grab towels from the bathroom. Wet a washcloth and bring everything in here." She whips out her phone and says, "Googling baby delivery here. The two of you get busy."

Shaking my head, I follow my brother from the room. We haven't cleared the hallway when he pushes me up against the wall and threatens me in a very low voice. "I love Shelby. If you bring shit here and endanger her, I'll kill you."

We don't have time for this shit. "There's a very small chance they'll discover what car I'm driving. Unless they stumble across the car itself, they won't trace me here. For Christ's sake, Linc. Kill me after the baby's born."

Lincoln's eyes hold fire. He loosens his grip and turns toward the kitchen. I locate the towels in the bathroom and carry them and a wet cloth back into the bedroom. Beth's pants and underwear rest at the bottom of the bed. There's a sheet pulled up to her waist. She gives me a small smile before she grits her teeth and bends slightly forward.

Linc walks back in, goes to the side of the bed, and takes Beth's hand. "Listen, sweetheart. I've never delivered a baby before but I'll get you through this." He takes the wet cloth from Shelby's hand and gently wipes Beth's brow. He reminds me of my father now that he's settled down—calm and controlled no matter the situation. I allow myself to pull in a long breath and unclench my fists.

Shelby starts reading directions aloud from the phone. "Do you need to push?" she asks.

Beth shakes her head and Linc slowly moves the sheet aside. "I'm going to check and see if we can see the baby's head, okay?" Her chin nods rapidly as tears slide down her face. Linc looks at me. "Come up here and hold her hand."

I take his place and he moves the sheet farther down. "I'm afraid for the baby," Beth cries.

I'm more afraid for her. "My brother and Shelby have this under control." I use the cloth Linc hands me to wipe her brow again. "I bought blankets for the baby and a cute little outfit she can wear after she's born."

Her grip on my hand tightens. "I need to push. God, I can't stop it."

Shelby moves a towel next to Beth's hip. The woman appears unfazed. "There's string and scissors in the bag. I'm going to drop them in the boiling water and I'll be right back." She leaves the room with one of the bags.

Beth's cry fills the room. Her face is filled with exertion. Things are moving so fast, but I'll never forget how beautiful she is at this moment as she brings a new life into the world. Death is cold and ugly. This is a miracle.

Shelby walks back in snapping directions like a drill sergeant.

"I can see the baby's head," Linc shouts. "Push with the next contraction and we'll see if he's ready to join us."

"She," Beth yells at him.

"Okay, she," he replies with an exasperated huff.

Beth's loud panting fills the room until her fingers relax on mine. I'm so damn proud of her for hanging on this long and keeping her cool. "Oh, God, oh, God," she cries out.

"Push, Beth," I tell her. Her response is unintelligible. Shelby runs out and returns with a bowl of steaming water and a towel wrapped around what must be the scissors and string.

"One more push," my brother encourages.

Beth's grip tightens and her scream causes the dog to begin howling in the hallway.

"Oh, my, so beautiful," Shelby whispers.

"If this is a girl, the world is changing faster than I can keep up with," Linc adds. The baby's cry shatters the room and we all laugh in relief.

"Take Beth's shirt and bra off so we can rest the baby on her chest," Shelby instructs me. "Google also says keeping the cord attached longer provides the baby with oxygen and iron. We need to wait at least two minutes."

"If it's on Google, it must be true," Linc mutters and receives a death glare from Shelby.

Beth wiggles to help me get her top and then bra off. My brother lifts the baby and places him face down on Beth's stomach and chest. "Here's your baby *boy*." He emphasizes "boy" with a smile. Beth's tears turn to sobs as she places her hands over the baby, who quiets now that he's back with his mother.

"To hell with two minutes, this is not what I was taught. Google has gone hippy," Linc grumbles to Shelby. "He'll bleed to death if we don't tie off the cord."

"You're an idiot. It says here that babies bleeding to death through the umbilical cord is an old wives' tale. They should call it an old fool's tale. There's some really good research to back up the oxygen and iron theory. What kind of research have you done on delivering babies?"

I want to use the umbilical cord to strangle them both. "I hate to tell the two of you this but I think you've argued through the two minutes."

My brother shrugs. "Can you roll the baby to his side?" he asks. I look at his tiny body and do nothing.

Shelby grasps the baby and rolls him enough so Linc can work. He starts crying again, which starts the dog howling. Within a few seconds, the dog actually drowns out the baby's cries.

"I'll quiet Daisy down. Don't forget to deliver the afterbirth." Shelby wets a rag and washes off her hands before walking to the bedroom door. "Come on, big boy, you need to go out back." The dog stops howling and goes to his belly. He doesn't budge when Shelby tugs his collar. "You stubborn goliath. If you weren't already neutered we'd be heading to the animal hospital tomorrow."

"Did she call him Daisy?" I chuckle as a way to keep my mind off Beth and the baby because my heart is doing flip flops.

"Don't ask," Linc replies while taking care of what I assume is the afterbirth. Babies are a bloody business and I'm relieved men don't deliver new life. Civilization would have ended long before it had a chance to start.

The baby fusses while my brother works. "Here," Link says and hands me the scissors. "You get to cut the cord." I take the scissors only because I'm not thinking straight.

I glance at Beth. Love shines from her eyes. She has so much faith in me and I'm finding it hard to breathe. My hands, which are always steady when pulling a trigger, shake. Linc has the cord tied off and without thinking it through, I cut between the strings as he directs. I look at the baby's face as soon as I make the snip. He's staring at me. His eyes are dark blue, nothing like his mother's, but his little nose is all Beth. I glance at Beth and she's watching me.

It's almost too much. All I can think of is escape. I've made so many mistakes in my life and closed far too many doors. Here is a woman who deserves a good father for her child. I'm the last person she should be looking at with such devotion.

"I have no idea what to name a boy," she says gently.

I fight to gain control of my shattered emotions. Humor is all I have. "He's going to look quite pretty in the pink outfit I bought him."

Beth smiles. I smile. The sound of the door closing makes me look away from her. My brother is gone and we're alone. I lean over Beth and kiss her cheek. For the first time in my life, I want something of my own. This woman, this child. I want to forget about vengeance and every bad thing I've done. I want to be the man who deserves Beth.

A few days ago all I could think of was death and finding the last two men on my list. Right at this moment, they're no longer important. This woman is. It's the biggest reason I need to find a safe place for her and the baby and disappear from their lives. I can't bring my dangerous world down on Beth.

"Will you prop the pillows up behind me?" she requests. She's so damn beautiful holding her son. The sheet is just beneath her hips and I move it up a bit. Beth lifts her son and I hand her a towel to wrap him in. She cradles him at her breasts and again I'm struck by the miracle of new life. His tiny fist moves to his mouth and sucking noises fill the quiet room.

"I've never done this before," she whispers while arranging the baby at her breast. She moves her nipple to his miniature mouth like a pro if I'm any judge. His tiny head makes small searching movements. Beth pinches her nipple and the baby finally grabs hold.

My heart is mush. "Angelo said I would never nurse my child." She glances up, her eyelashes wet with tears. "Thank you, Rack."

How do I let this woman go?

Chapter Eighteen

Beth

Diapers were on the list I gave Rack. I've never put a diaper on a newborn or realized how hard it is. Rack watches helplessly and I can see he's further out of his comfort zone than I am. I figure out which way the diaper goes and slide it beneath his tiny bottom. The last thing I expect is the stream of warm pee that sprays upward and soaks me. Rack hands me a towel from the stack on the edge of the bed.

His lips curve up in a shameless smile. "It's never too early to teach shooting straight."

"Thanks, I think he's got it down," I say with a laugh. I finish attaching the small tabs. As first diapers go it's a disaster of slightly crooked proportions.

I gaze at my son and feel such overwhelming love—lopsided diaper and all. Before giving birth I refused to consider having a boy. Now, within two hours of his arrival, I can't imagine anything else. Linc loaned me a button shirt so I can breastfeed. He blushed when he brought it in, which I thought humorous. He's seen everything there is to see and now he blushes.

I'm tired, filled with joy, and terrified in equal measures. I was protective over the baby before he was born. Now, the need to keep him safe has tripled. Angelo will never get his hands on my son.

As soon as the baby falls asleep, I ask Rack if he'll bring Shelby in to help me clean up. I washed the baby with the water Shelby left and now he's wrapped snuggly in one of the blankets Rack purchased. He leaves to find Shelby. I can't quite put my finger on why Rack is acting so strange. He's quieter than usual for sure. He hasn't held the baby or asked to. Linc did for a short time. He called him a little bugger and told him he would make a great police officer someday. From the corner of my eye I watched Rack turn away and stare at the wall.

I'm sure seeing a woman give birth can't be pretty from a single man's perspective. I glance down at the sleeping bundle in my arms. This isn't Rack's baby and I'm not Rack's wife. He's here because he's brave and honorable. It doesn't matter how bad I want him, I need to mentally keep Rack out of the daddy role. But, what if?

Shelby sticks her head in and I wave her over. "Will you help me clean up?" I ask in embarrassment. Everyone in the house has seen every part of me and maybe parts I've never seen, but now that the birth is over, I'm feeling shy. I just don't think I can do it myself. My babyless tummy looks like I haven't given birth yet.

"Sure. I looked through the bags but didn't find any pads. I have some at my place. Let me run next door and grab them."

I never thought of pads. A small smile escapes me thinking of Rack buying them. He'd handle it as he does everything else. The man comes through in any situation and makes you think he's done it a million times before.

You're giving birth. No problem! We'll get you to my brother and he'll deliver the baby.

I suddenly remember Shelby is waiting patiently for my answer. "Sure and thank you."

"No, thank you. That was the most incredible thing I've witnessed. Truly a miracle." Her glowing smile says it all.

She closes the door and I'm alone with my son. I'm having trouble keeping my eyes open, but I refuse to sleep. I stare at his tiny fingers, button nose, and perfect everything. I don't see his father in his features, but even if I did it wouldn't matter. I kiss his soft forehead and the top of his head. He's my miracle.

According to the bedside clock, it's ten minutes before Shelby returns. "Sorry about that," she says after closing the door behind her. "I have warm, soapy water for you. We'll give you a bed bath and change the towels beneath you too."

"I love you," I say quietly so I don't wake the baby.

She laughs, leaves the bowl with water on the nightstand, and walks from the room again. She's back in under a minute with my clothes from the car. Between the two of us we manage to get me washed up and I feel so much better. More tired than I've ever been but at least content.

"How's Daisy? That's her name, right?"

"He. Daisy's a male. I'm sure he's still pacing like an expectant father. He loves children and when you're comfortable with it, we'll let him have a peek. A baby doesn't need a heavy dose of dog slobber on his first day in the world, so we'll give it some time." She holds up the pink jumper Rack purchased. "We'll take pictures and show them to him when he's a teenager," she says as she laughs.

I don't know where the emotion comes from but it wells up in my chest and I lose it. Tears turn to sobs before I can control myself. "We d-don't have-have pictures of him," I stutter between breaths.

Shelby's smile is soft with understanding. "That's easy to fix." She slides her cell from her pocket and starts snapping until I stop crying and laugh at her goofiness. She takes photo after photo. I pull aside the blanket and tuck the baby against my chest so his little diapered bottom sticks in the air. Shelby keeps pressing the button on her phone. He sleeps through most of it.

"You're a goof," I say when she has me hold up each foot and she zooms in.

"A complete goof. At least Linc loves me exactly as I am." Her eyes shine when she says it and I envy their relationship. "The guys brought my rocking chair over. I figure we can place it in here by the bed and take turns rocking the baby while you try to sleep. Rutherford..." she says and looks at me questionably. "Rack?" she corrects and I nod. "He's about ready to drop or so Linc says. I'm not sure if he should take a shift until tomorrow."

"You and Linc must be tired too?"

"I'm good. Linc is taking tomorrow off work and it won't kill me to skip a day of classes. I have a friend who had a baby six months ago. I'll go to her place in a few hours and see what she can scrape together for the baby. Does that work for you?"

I'm not sure what to say. Linc and Shelby could be in danger with us here. I also don't know what Rack's told them. The pain kept me from following most of the conversations when we arrived.

Shelby breaks into my thoughts. "No worries. Linc and Rack are planning a course of action. I'm aware there's someone looking for you. I'm the fiancée of a cop. This is our life. I'll make up a story to tell my friend. The guys also think I shouldn't go to the store and go hog wild on new baby items like I want to. That's put a huge damper on spoiling this little guy." She slides her hand over the baby's back and some little bird tells me that once she marries Lincoln, babies will be in their very near future.

Saying thank you feels so inadequate and tears fill my eyes again. I guess it takes a while for the hormones to level out because I've never cried this much in my life.

"No more of that. Between the guys and Daisy, you're safer here than any place on earth."

I don't doubt her.

"I'll go tell the men they can move the rocking chair in here so you can sleep."

"If you don't mind, leave the chair out there and bring Rack in here to sleep. I trust you to keep the baby safe while we rest. But bring him back when he needs to eat or you need a break."

She actually claps her hands like an excited child. "Daisy is the best guard dog imaginable. He might not look it but that dog can sense danger and has no problem taking care of business. I'll get Rack in here before I whip that bundle of joy from your arms and hug his little body for the next few hours. I'm dying to hold him."

I look down at my son and my heart melts all over again.

Rack enters a minute later. Shelby's right. He looks exhausted.

"Lay down with me. Shelby will hold the baby while we sleep."

He carefully slides onto the bed beside me. He leans his head on his hand. "You're beautiful," he says sleepily.

I ignore the words because he's hallucinating. "He's perfect, Rack. I knew you would take care of us."

He starts to say something but stops. "He's perfect like his mother. He also needs a name."

Names have been drifting in and out of my mind. "Can he just be *the baby* for now? I'm too tired to decide and he'll be stuck with his name forever."

Rack just smiles at me and slowly blinks.

Shelby pops her head in. "You ready for me to take over aunty duties?"

"Sure." Shelby's wonderful and even during the heat of childbirth, she remained calm and controlled.

"I'll bring him back when he's ready to eat. Get some sleep and don't worry about a thing," she says as she takes him from my arms.

I'm bereft and almost beg her to hand him back. But I need sleep. Rack needs sleep. Shelby will care for him. She closes the door behind her. Rack removes his shirt and then crawls into bed with me. He turns off the lamp. "Come here," he whispers and pulls me into his arms. "Sleep," he says softly against my hair once I'm situated.

And just like that, I fall asleep.

It seems like it's only been minutes, when the baby's crying wakes me up. Shelby opens the door and strides in. I squint into the room when Rack turns on the light. "I'm sorry, two hours is all he lasted," she murmurs. I unbutton the shirt and lift my arms. "I'll be back in about thirty minutes," she says over the baby's cries.

Rack helps position pillows behind me. The baby starts sucking as soon as I cradle him and push my nipple to his mouth. He makes slurping noises and he fists the skin of my breast while he eats. I'm fully aware of Rack watching. Maybe I should feel uncomfortable but I don't.

Rack laughs at a particularly loud slurp. "He's a hungry little tiger."

The baby fidgets a few minutes later. "I think I'm supposed to burp him." I lift him to my shoulder and gently pat his back. The blanket is falling off and Rack helps remove it.

"Yeah, fella, the pink needs to go. We'll find you a nice football jersey at the first opportunity," he says at the sight of the pink sleeper that's two sizes too big.

I can't stop my smile. "I didn't know you liked football."

Rack's eyes stay glued to the baby. "All men like football."

No way on earth will I argue with his statement.

Chapter Nineteen

Rack

I can't sort out the rambling thoughts in my head. I know what to do with anger and aggression. I've handled both more times than I care to count. These thoughts are different. Watching Beth nurse the baby is the loveliest, sexiest, and most precious thing I've ever witnessed. Not that I'm thinking sex while watching. No. I'm thinking family, settling down, and changing my life. It's a joke I can't laugh about. I've done too many terrible things and I'm not finished. Not even close.

"You've got it bad, brother mine," Linc says while rocking the baby. The child I haven't held because even thinking about it makes my stomach twist into knots. There's this yawning hole in my heart and if I touch him I don't know if I could ever let go.

Linc is destined to be a father. He'll be wonderful at it—a great husband, drive a minivan, and do his best, even with his job, to never miss one of his kid's games. Our father did the same. If Linc wasn't holding the baby, I swear I'd deck him.

Yes, I have it bad, no denying it. I want it all and I want to erase the last few years. I want Andrew and Nick back. I want to be the man Beth and the baby need. It's an unattainable dream. I deal in reality and I need to somehow stop the longing that's tearing me apart.

I glance into my brother's dark eyes. There's so much left unsaid between us. Hell. There's so much left unsaid between me and my entire family. They were safer out of my life and now I've brought Linc roaring into this crisis. It was unfair of me. Only days ago I'd have sworn it would never happen. Beth and her needs quickly tore down the safety net I placed around my family.

I look away. "I have it bad," I agree.

He grunts. "Bad enough to settle down and stop the bullshit you've been up to?" His words are clipped but soft because of the baby.

I've been expecting this. "You don't understand," I say in frustration and begin pacing the floor.

His face goes an angry shade of red. "No, I don't. Neither do Cal and Woody. Fuck, our parents don't understand. Why is that, Rutherford? Why don't you explain it to me?" Linc's anger is evident. It's not the time for this discussion, but will there ever be a time?

"The men who killed Andrew needed to pay..."

Linc holds one hand up and keeps me from finishing the statement. "Don't you fucking tell me you've killed people." He stops and readjusts his hold on the baby. His voice lowers. "I'm a cop for Christ's sake."

Right at this moment I'd give anything to be holding Beth's child. The pain is all-consuming. Just once. Would that really make it so hard to leave him behind? Leave Beth behind? The answer is yes. This is not my son even though, with every part of my soul, I want him to be. Hell, he doesn't need to be my blood for me to take him under my wing and raise him.

Then I ask myself...raise him to be what? A criminal? A killer? I can't do it, won't do it.

With a loud frustrated sigh I look back at my brother. "What do you think war is, Linc? Of course I've killed people. More people than I can count. I pointed my rifle at the enemy and sprayed bullets."

Linc's eyes burn into mine. "You know that's not what I'm fucking saying."

God, I want to strangle him. "The men who killed Andrew don't play by your rules. They kill indiscriminately. The only way to stop them and others like them is to take them out. Mexican drug lords are similar to Middle Eastern terrorists, except these guys are on our doorstep pushing into our territory."

Linc laughs with derision. "You talk like a drug dealer. Hell, you work for a drug dealer. Do you feed yourself this shit so you're okay with what you do?"

"You know nothing about the man I work for," I spit out. Burning anger starts coiling in my gut.

"So tell me." He rocks a little faster in the chair. "Tell me so I understand."

He'll never understand but I try anyway. "The men I work with have a different definition of right and wrong. They make their own laws. Good or bad, the people in that world understand their laws. The men who killed Andrew have no line they won't cross. They do worse than kill border patrol officers. They kill women and children." I glance down at the worn carpet. "They smash children's skulls against brick walls, they rape women and mutilate them if they don't kill them outright. And," I meet my brother's eyes and see him grimace, "they rape young girls—ten, eleven, twelve—still babies. This isn't a fight for peacekeepers like you and Cal and Woody. It's a fight for killers. The war taught me to kill and I'm damned good at it. Moon and Gomez feel the same way I do. Moon can't stop the tide of drugs pouring into this country but he can make sure they aren't laced with poison and they don't get into the hands of children." I sit down across from my brother and lean my head against the cushion behind my head. "You're a good man, Linc. You'll never understand."

He remains quiet for a long time. In the stillness my attention turns to a colorful wall clock with large hands that ticks loudly. The entire house is out of character for my brother. I see Shelby's influence everywhere. There's a sheer red scarf hanging from a lamp. I'm happy for him. He was always so serious. Shelby has softened him. Not toward me but in so many other ways.

"Where do Beth and this baby fit into this life you've made?"

It's so simple and still so damn hard. "She doesn't. She has no idea who or what I am. She's running from a mob boss's son. The last thing she needs is getting involved with a man who works for a different mob."

"You work for the Mob?" Beth whispers from the hallway.

I turn. Her devastated expression guts me. Before I answer, she walks over and takes the baby from my brother. She's blinking back tears. I stare into her eyes when she turns to me and I see everything I deserve—anger, fear, and the worst...betrayal.

Daisy's whine breaks the silence. "I'll take Daisy next door and give the two of you time alone," my brother says after grabbing Daisy's collar.

There will never be enough time to make this right with Beth.

She takes Linc's place in the rocking chair after the front door closes. Condemnation shines from her eyes. "I should have asked sooner," she states. "Who are you, Rack?" She continues before I can answer. "Hell, I should have asked Angelo that question too."

I watch her with the baby. So protective, such an incredible mother. She deserves the truth and I told her I would never lie to her. "I work for an Arizona and New Mexico crime lord. Nowhere close to the level as the Gimonde family." Beth repositions the baby so he's upright and against her chest. Her hand gently rubs his back over the blanket. "I swore I'd tell you whatever you wanted to know."

She looks away. "Why?"

Her discovering who I am and what I do was inevitable. That doesn't mean it's any easier to explain. "I'm searching for the men who killed my brother. The organization I work for helps me and I help them." She shakes her head and I keep talking. "I kill and torture people. I get rid of the bodies when needed. I've transported drugs and guns. I make no excuses. I'm a dangerous man and that's exactly what you needed to get away from Gimonde. I won't make excuses for that. I'll find a safe place for you and the baby. You'll be done with me." I lean forward and rest my elbows on my knees. "He needs a birth certificate and you need a new last name. The man I work for will make it happen."

Beth's gaze shifts to the floor. She speaks so low I can't make out what she says. Tears fall to the carpet. I can't take it. I cross to the rocking chair, go to my knees, and wrap my arm around her shoulder. "How could I let this happen again?" she asks desperately. She's right and so incredibly wrong. I'm the only person who can keep her safe. Her next words kill me a little more. "Nick would hate who you've become."

My fingers slide beneath her chin and I tip her head so our eyes meet. Tears hang on her lashes. "You're wrong. Nick would understand. He would have done anything to keep you safe and he would have killed anyone who hurt you."

She gulps in a breath. "He would hate me too."

I want to shake her for sounding so defeated. "Nick could never hate you."

"You're wrong." Her expression is condemning, so her next words surprise me. "I love you," she says simply and yet it's anything but simple.

I say nothing. She can't love me.

She shakes off my arm, stands, and walks away with the baby. I don't stop her. Her hero worship is shattered. What she feels is not love and I'm as far from a hero as anyone can be.

Chapter Twenty

Beth

Pillows are behind my back and I'm nursing my hungry son. My nipples are sore, but I don't care. I crave this closeness and need the comfort it brings.

Part of me wishes I hadn't listened to Rack and Linc's conversation. I'm incredibly foolish when it comes to men. It never occurred to me that Rack was anyone other than who my brother wrote me about—a good, solid man. Now I'm back to square one—in too far over my head with no way out.

Rack doesn't believe I love him. Why should he? He has no idea I see him through my brother's eyes. Nick conveyed his respect for Rack in every email he sent. It was easy for me to fantasize and turn Rack into a mythical god. It was so easy to form a crush on the man my brother handpicked. Nick made it clear that Rack was perfect for me. Then I met Kevin, a real person and not just some fantasy guy my brother gushed over.

I was angry with my brother too. Angry that he re-enlisted and returned for another tour of duty. Rebelling against Nick's amazing friend who he wanted me to meet was easy. I had a flesh and blood man to take his place, or so I thought. Kevin never wanted to marry me. When Nick died, Kevin didn't know any other way to bring me out of my grief. Truthfully, a ring helped. Maybe someday I will forgive him for sleeping with my best friend. Our relationship was a sham, our engagement more so. I see that now. I think my anger derives from what happened after Kevin. That being Angelo and the mess I made there. In all this there's one common denominator…me. Bad choice after bad choice.

My son yawns and then grasps my nipple again, causing me to inhale sharply. Shelby and I researched breastfeeding on the Internet and discovered the discomfort is common. Time will cure the problem and Shelby promised to bring home some breast cream today. I'll survive and be thankful for the opportunity to feed my son. His beautiful eyes flutter and he grins, in his perfect little newborn way, around my nipple. How do you express something greater than love? I don't think you can.

"We have each other, little man," I whisper and squeeze him a tiny bit tighter. I'll make sure it's enough. I need to keep my heart in check and discover how to fall out of love with Rack. "No more men," I say and then smile because that's all you can do when you're looking at something so precious.

Shelby knocks softly and enters the room a short time later. She brings in a box, places it on the floor by the bed, and hands me a small bag. I look inside and see the breast cream.

"My friend said you can rewash the clothes if you want but she did it before putting them in plastic a few weeks ago when she cleaned out her son's dresser."

I sniff.

"Are you okay?"

I take a breath and gain control. "I'll be fine. Rack and I chased Linc off. Is he back?"

She shakes her head. "Rack said Linc's at my place with Daisy. I figured Daisy got a little too rambunctious. My house is the other half of the duplex if you haven't figured that out."

I can't help asking. "Did you know Rack is a criminal?"

Shelby moves to the side of the bed and puts her hand on my arm. "Oh, sweetie." She smiles sadly. "I know Linc. I also know his other two brothers and their parents. Rack has made bad decisions. No man who rescued you and loves this little guy could be all bad."

I gaze down at my son—his chubby, rosy cheeks. His tiny fingers curled into fists. His lips that make sucking motions even though he's sleeping. It breaks my heart to say the words, "Rack doesn't love him. He's another man's child."

Shelby sighs heavily. "Keep telling yourself that. Watch his expression when he looks at the baby. If that isn't love, I don't know what is."

Shelby lives in a fantasy world if she thinks Rack loves my son. I change the subject because this one is too painful. "I need a name and nothing fits."

She knows exactly what I'm doing and bites her lip before giving in. "No worries. You'll find the right name. These things can't be rushed. How about we get this little boy in some proper clothes and take some more pictures?"

I love the pink jumper. Rack bought it. I blink away more tears. I hate the damn hormones that bring on these waterworks. We change his diaper first, which makes him angry. He's asleep again before we finish. I'm a pro now at diaper changes and handle it easily. We put him in a thin, white, one-piece sleeper with small colorful images of baseballs covering it. Rack steps in just as we're fastening the last snaps on the new sleeper.

Rack has been nothing but self-assured since rescuing me. That's not the expression on his face now. He's hesitant and I wonder if he thinks I'll tell him to leave the room. He saved us. I can't imagine how my baby's life would have turned out without Rack's help.

"Do you want to hold him?" I ask. The lines in Rack's face relax and I see relief.

He shakes his head. I cast a quick *I told you so* glance at Shelby. Daisy sticks his large head in the room and gives a low whine.

"You need to eat, Daisy. Let's go, you can see the baby later." Shelby walks around Rack and turns at the door. "My friend gave you a swing and bassinet too. There's not enough room in here for both. I'll have Linc set up the swing in the living room. I'll bring something in for both of you to munch on after I feed Daisy."

I don't want to be alone with Rack. I told him I love him, which was really stupid. No man wants to hear a woman say that after a few days. "We'll come out there to eat. I need to get out of the bedroom and move around."

"Twenty minutes," Shelby replies before closing the door and leaving us alone.

An unraveled stitch in the comforter catches my interest. Rack's on the opposite side of the bed from where I'm lying and he's still too close. Like my brother, Rack is larger than life. He's also sexy and even a woman who's just given birth can't deny it.

"What has you so amused?" Rack asks, and I realize I must have smiled.

I run my finger over the thread again before looking up. He's moved to the end of the bed and he's watching me. His eyes are hypnotic and the ache inside me doubles. I do love him even though I know it won't work between us. I need to speak my mind and get it over with. "You rescued us. I can never repay you. I owe you so much and at the same time I'm incredibly conflicted."

"After you're safe, you'll never see me again. You'll have a new life and you'll meet someone who is the right man for you." He looks away before meeting my gaze again. "Someone Nick would approve of."

Nick approved of Rack.

"Have you thought of a name?" Rack asks.

The baby's name comes out of nowhere. "I like Carson."

Rack thinks about it for a moment before nodding.

"Carson Andrew," I add.

Rack closes his eyes. His arms flex and his hands fist. There is so much pain in his eyes when he opens them. "It's a wonderful name." He shoves his hands into his pockets and glances around the room.

I have no doubt he loved his brother as much as I loved mine. I never felt the need to hunt down the men who killed Nick. That's the major difference between the two of us. I just wanted my brother back and the pain of his loss to go away.

"I think it's a wonderful name too. Tell me something about your brother so I can pass the story to Carson when he's older." Maybe if Rack talks about his brother he can release some of the anger he still carries over his death.

Rack sits on the corner of the bed and gathers his thoughts. "Andrew hated bread crust. My mom cut the crust off all his sandwiches from the time he was a toddler. Andrew was sixteen when I left for my first tour of duty. Mom wanted to have a quiet going away party, so I came over for lunch. My mom made Andrew's sandwich without the crust. When she left the room we teased him non-stop." Rack looks down at the baby. "If Carson doesn't like crust, it stops at ten. Those are guy rules." Rack's eyes are haunted even with the humor of his story. My heart aches for him.

"Guy rules, huh?" I challenge lightly. "Why didn't Andrew tell your mother to stop?"

Just the corner of Rack's lips tip into a smile. "You don't know my mom. She would shake her head, mutter something in Italian, and keep doing it because it pleased her. She's a horrible cook, so when we were lucky enough to have sandwiches, we ate them gladly."

"Italian and didn't cook. That's awful."

"Oh, she cooked, which was worse."

I can't help laughing and Rack smiles back. "You ready to go eat?" He nods at the door.

"I'm starving."

And my heart is aching and I'm dying inside.

Chapter Twenty-One

Rack

I sleep beside Beth the following two nights. We don't speak about her future and she never mentions the sleeping arrangements. I would move to the couch if she insisted. I lie to myself by thinking it's safer for me to be in the room with her. So much remains unsaid and maybe that's how our relationship will end.

The baby sleeps next to the bed in a bassinet. The downside is that I lay awake longer than I should thinking about what it would be like if this were really my life. A wife, a child. A dream I never imagined. I only close my eyes when I'm too exhausted to keep them open.

On day four at my brother's house, I take my throwaway cell into the backyard and sit on the steps while Daisy does his business. He's one of the oddest looking dogs imaginable with shepherd markings and the kinky curly hair of a standard poodle. The day after we arrived, Daisy and I had a serious problem when he tried humping my leg. Linc, the ass, snickered. Shelby stopped me from pummeling my brother by saying Daisy really liked the Street brothers and unless we proved who the boss is, Daisy's "like" might result in puppies.

Shelby's a strange one. Her dog more so.

I explained the situation to Daisy and we reached a mutual understanding. He won't hump my leg and I won't shoot him. Beth laughed throughout *the talk*. Daisy gave a huff, settled down on the floor, and follows the new rules to the letter. Later that night, after the women went to bed, Linc told me Daisy saved Shelby when a killer attacked her. It only reaffirmed that Daisy needs strict guidance more than a bullet.

I watch Daisy explore the yard for a few minutes before tapping Gomez's number into the phone. He answers on the third ring.

"Hola," I say.

"At least you're alive, fucker."

"Alive and in need of a favor."

No hesitation. "Name it."

"Paperwork for a woman and a baby boy."

He whistles. "Gimonde senior is looking for her now too. He's not happy with his son. Senior will protect her and the baby. He's given his word to Moon."

I shouldn't be surprised. "Won't happen. I'm going after his son."

Gomez is silent for a few seconds. He knows Angelo's days are now numbered. "We're between a rock and a fucking hard place," he finally replies.

I hate bringing Gomez and Moon into this but I've drawn the line. "I won't allow Gimonde to be a threat and that includes senior. It's on me. Put out the word that I've gone rogue. Beth and the baby need to disappear or I wouldn't ask you for this favor."

"Understood. Consider it done. It will take a few days and we'll need a picture of the woman and—"

"Beth," I say before I can stop myself. Even I can hear the way I say her name.

Gomez misses nothing. It's what keeps him alive. "Like that is it?"

"Hell." I don't say anything for a moment. Gomez waits me out. "I'll make sure she's safe and then she'll be out of my life. My world is no place for her and the baby."

He chuckles. "Yeah, keep telling yourself that. Didn't work for me and I don't see it working for you."

Gomez sent Celina away for six months. He was miserable but would have kept her safe and stayed away if she hadn't come back on her own. "No offense but Beth has a baby to protect and she'll do whatever it takes to keep him safe."

He grunts. "Moon is unhappy about all of this. He's willing to take on Gimonde."

"I hope you've talked fucking sense into him."

Gomez's full laugh explodes in my ear. "Moon does what the fuck he wants and I protect his ass after the fact. You know that as well as I do."

"He'll lose and now that Mak and Celina are in the picture you have other priorities just as I do."

"You worry about your woman and we'll worry about ours. Gimonde senior won't let this go. He'll never stop hunting you."

"He can hunt me in Mexico, then. He won't be the only one."

"I'll call this number when the papers are ready. Take a picture and text it with names."

Our conversation is over but I hold the line. "Thank you, Alex." I rarely use his first name. There are so many other things I should say. Moon and Gomez pulled me from self-destruction and gave me focus. I owe them everything.

He ends the call without responding. Typical Gomez.

Beth and the baby sleep more than anything. I spend hours working out in my brother's living room now that Linc and Shelby have returned to work. I cook for Beth but don't help her with Carson. She never complains.

I've avoided her when she nurses Carson, especially since her milk came in. Her breasts practically bust the seams of my brother's shirts. I can't take it even though I know I'm a shit for having sexual thoughts over a woman's milk-engorged breasts.

I'm stuck in limbo knowing this can't last and praying it will.

Thirty-six hours after talking to Gomez he calls in the middle of the night and our world changes again. "Are you at your brother's?" is the first thing he asks.

"Fuck," I swear while sitting up and grabbing my gun from the bedside table.

"Stay put. Dax is on his way to escort you to his place. Does your brother have somewhere safe to go?"

"Hell, I don't know." Beth places her hand on my shoulder. Our cozy quiet time is at an end.

"Dax can leave some of his men behind."

I put my hand over Beth's. "Let me talk to my brother. Do you know how they found out about my past?"

"Not yet but we will."

I have no doubt that whoever ratted me out will pay. You don't betray Moon, and the last person you want handing down punishment is Gomez.

We end the call.

"Gimonde knows we're here. We have a few hours. My boss is sending friends to get us." I sleep in my cargo pants so I only need to pull on my shirt. "Angelo's dad says he'll protect you and the baby from his son."

"No, he's lying. Angelo spoke of his father endlessly. The man is no different than his son." Conviction is in every clipped word. I'm glad it's settled. If Gimonde senior comes after her, he'll be as dead as his son will be once I have Beth safe.

I walk to the door, turn around, and see her pulling pants up her legs. She's been sleeping in my brother's endless supply of shirts. The only thing that saves me is the fact she just had a baby. I couldn't have handled being in the same bed and not touching her otherwise. "I need to talk to my brother."

She glances over her shoulder. "Go." She's in full mother tiger mode.

The *talk* with Linc goes as well as I expected. It ends with me sitting in the living room with my head back trying to keep my bloody nose from making a mess. I refused to defend myself because I completely understand his anger. Beth, the baby, and Shelby are next door. They'll stay on Shelby's side of the duplex until Dax arrives. Dax is another thing my brother's angry about.

Dax is the president of Desert Crows, an outlaw motorcycle club in Arizona. They have close ties with Moon's organization but it's not widely known. If Gimonde gets anywhere near the Crows' compound, Dax and his men will defend their territory to the death.

My brother is storming through his house collecting everything that belongs to Shelby and boxing it. If Gimonde's men come here, he doesn't want them to know he has a woman. I tried to help and almost got a black eye to go with the bloody nose. I deserve his rage. The only thing keeping him from killing me is Beth and the baby. He knows this was their only chance. He just doesn't like it.

He finishes boxing Shelby's things and walks back into the living room. He doesn't say anything for several minutes while he paces. "You know I need to call Mom and Dad. If Gimonde knows about our connection, he knows about our parents."

"Yeah, Wood and Calvin too," I add.

"Do you have any idea what you've done to Mom? This will crush her all over again."

I don't answer. I've never forgotten my family, but I let them go thinking I would never see them again. Saying I'm sorry isn't enough. And truthfully I'm not sorry. Andrew was my brother and his death hit everyone hard. I would do it all again.

"The car," I think aloud. "I need to get rid of it so it's not discovered here."

Linc stops and turns toward me. "You said it's legal."

His tone pisses me off. "The damn thing is legal, paid cash but didn't register it."

"I'll hide it in impound. We can't find cars in there half the time as it is."

His words turn the shield I wrapped around myself when I separated from my family to dust. I've turned Linc's life to shit and he's still willing to help me.

Chapter Twenty-Two

Beth

Carson is fussy. Hell, I'm fussy. I have no control and it's like being at the ranch all over again.

Rack is delivering me into the hands of a motorcycle gang. A very bad one. He didn't pull punches when he told me who and what they are.

I walk back and forth over the cool tile floor and bounce Carson against my chest.

"I'll walk with him if you need to sleep."

I turn to Shelby, who's been nothing but wonderful. Now I've brought danger straight to her doorstep. "I'll sleep in the car after we leave. I'm sure Carson will sleep then or at least I hope." I've tried everything to get him to nap. Not even feeding works.

She wipes the edges of her eyes. "We'll miss you," she says as she bends down and pets Daisy.

I stop walking. "I'm so sorry, Shelby."

She stands and crosses the space between us. Her arms wrap around me and Carson. "Don't ever be sorry, we'll be okay. All you think about is this, sweetheart." She pulls back and smiles "Now hand him over and let's see if Aunt Shelby can calm this fussy boy down."

She places Carson against her chest and rubs his back while walking back and forth. "There, there," she singsongs.

Keys rattle at the front door and my heart stops. Linc pushes it open and carries a box inside. "I'll put this and the others in the spare room," he says to Shelby in a clipped tone.

He's angry, as he should be. I feel horrible. Shelby is too damn nice. Linc understands the danger I've placed them in. I remain quiet and sit on the couch while Shelby walks Carson. The baby grows fussier and his cries turn to full out screams with little huffs of trembling breaths thrown in. Linc leaves and returns a few minutes later with another box. I'm about to stand and take Carson back when Linc speaks up.

"Give me the little guy," he says. Shelby hands Carson over and we both watch in bafflement when the baby quiets a few seconds after Linc cuddles him against his shoulder.

Shelby smiles. "It's the big manly chests that do it. Women and babies are highly susceptible."

Linc winks at me.

Carson's eyes drift closed and Linc steps closer to me. "This isn't your fault, Beth, so don't blame yourself. My brother will take care of you and see you're safe. I'll keep Shelby safe." His grin expands when he glances at Shelby. "Even if she thinks she can do it alone and proven she's more than capable, I won't allow anyone to touch her."

Shelby smiles back and they're caught in a private moment. Shelby told me their story last night while the brothers watched a baseball game on TV. Their romance was funny, dangerous, and exciting. I want a love story just like theirs.

A few minutes later, Linc hands a sleeping Carson back to me.

"One more box and all the crap is gone from my place."

"Hey," Shelby says. Linc winks at me again and walks out.

Shelby and I wait on the couch. My eyes drift closed. I feel like all I've done is sleep for days. I never dreamed giving birth takes this much out of you. Rack's voice wakes me. I glance around and Shelby is no longer in the room.

"They're here. I have a car seat for the baby. Change and feed him and then we need to go." He's in protection mode again. Gone is the relaxed Rack. This is Rack the killer.

I resituate the baby, pull up the first T-shirt I've worn in days, and unclip one of the nursing bras Shelby's friend gave me. Carson is tired but latches on when I position him. I grimace and take a few deep breaths. Rack hasn't watched me nurse the last two days and he gives me a quizzical look. I ignore it by changing the subject. "Do I have time to say goodbye to Shelby or are they gone?"

His eyes lift from my breast and I almost laugh when he gives me a guilty look. "They're still here," he says and turns to look out the window.

Is feeling desirable something you want when a man watches you breastfeed? Heat travels to my cheeks and my question is answered. I'm still carrying baby weight and will for months, my breasts look like they will explode milk half the time, and I've barely taken time to comb my hair. Makeup is an elusive dream. All that doesn't matter because yes, I want to be desirable to this man.

I peer down at the baby. He's not hungry. Now that he's settled down he just wants to sleep. He grumbles a bit when I change him but that's it. My stomach is in knots. Rack is placing me in the hands of a motorcycle gang.

"I promise you'll be safe. Trust me!" I'm not surprised he reads my expression. I do trust him but I hate feeling out of control.

A few minutes later, we walk out the door. There's an ordinary compact car in the driveway and no motorcycles in sight. I turn in the direction of Linc's front door. He and Shelby walk outside. Shelby sprints over and throws her arms around me and Carson. She's crying. We know this is it. We'll never see each other again and neither of us can contain our tears. I pull away and throw my arms around Linc next. "Thank you so much." It's completely inadequate. He squeezes gently and kisses my cheek. I pull away and glance down at Daisy, who's whining like crazy. I pat his head knowing I'll miss him too. "I'll find Carson a big sweetie just like you," I tell Daisy.

Shelby takes Carson from my arms and breathes in his scent before kissing his nose. With one final kiss, she hands him over. This goodbye is harder than I imagined. Linc pulls Shelby into his arms, which is my cue that it's time. I turn and follow Rack to the car before I turn into a blubbering mess.

There's an older man in the front passenger seat. I situate Carson in his new car seat, walk around the other side, and get in the back. Rack folds himself behind the wheel.

The stranger peers around the seat. "Ma'am. Name's Curly Sue, friends call me Curly." His beard is long and shaggy, his head shaved. Faded tattoos cover the arm I can see. God, I think one of the tattoos is a swastika. What the hell is Rack thinking?

Curly turns around and Rack pulls the car out. I look back and Shelby's waving at me. I wave until I no longer see her. I dig in the diaper bag, which is on the floorboard beneath the car seat, and find tissue to blow my nose.

Twenty minutes later we pull onto the highway and a few motorcycles pull in behind us. Ten minutes later a few more join the pack. Including Curly, our escort is nine strong. My life has gone from a cheating fiancé to becoming pregnant by a mob boss's son to a skinhead motorcycle gang escorting me to safety.

This isn't the rabbit hole. It's the River Styx leading to hell.

Chapter Twenty-Three

Rack

I know Beth is worried, but she hangs in like a trouper. I told her a little about the Crows. Two years ago their help wouldn't be an option. Each man riding behind us has spent time in prison. None of them transitioned easily. When Dax took over as president of the club, he had just rescued a child from being sold on the black market by the man he killed to gain leadership of the club. That child is the niece of the woman Gomez fell in love with. Without Dax's help, I've no doubt the child would be dead now.

After Dax killed the president of the Crows, he made sweeping changes. The biggest being acceptance of the Latina woman he fell in love with and married. You toe the line and follow Dax's rules or you become part of the Arizona desert terrain in an unmarked grave. Dax and his club might be slightly domesticated now but the way they deal with trouble is similar to Moon's approach and I don't see that changing.

Gomez is indebted to Dax for saving Celina's niece, and Dax is indebted to Moon and Gomez for standing behind him throughout the difficult transition of his club. Now Moon and the Crows are in business together. Moon is a silent backer in Dax's medical marijuana dispensaries. If the legal marijuana law passes in the next election, Moon's organization and the entire club will make a shitload more of legal money. As an ex-con, Dax and his crew can't have their name on the dispensaries. That's where Dax's wife, Sofia, comes in. The woman is as business savvy as they come and has a clean record. She's also a mean, protective mamma bear, and no one in the club tangles with her unless they want to feel her claws.

Beth will calm down once she meets Sofia and the twins. The two women should get along just fine. We'll be temporarily safe at the clubhouse. I'll get my shit together and take the next step from there.

The baby starts fussing three hours into our trip. We're halfway to the clubhouse. Curly calls Dax and tells him we're pulling into the next rest stop.

"Shhhh, sweetie. Mommy promises to feed you in just a few minutes."

Beth's soothing has little effect and Carson's cries fill the car until they're one long scream. I take the rest stop exit and Beth removes Carson from his car seat as soon as I park.

"Kid's got a healthy set of lungs on 'im." Curly laughs in his thick crusty smoker's voice. He steps out of the car and waits for the bikes to park.

"I'll be back in a minute, I need to speak with Dax." Beth gives me a frazzled look and nods. I step outside and walk to Dax. He throws his arms around me and lifts me off my feet. I'm a few inches taller and weigh more, so it's no easy feat.

"Put me down, you hog," I tell him.

My feet hit the pavement and I slap him on the back. "Thank you, Dax. Sorry to take you away from your family."

"No man, never be sorry. Things were getting boring in my neck of the desert and we needed a run with a little excitement thrown in." *Hell yeah* and a few grunts from the other men accompany his words.

I glance toward the car, where Beth is feeding the baby, and then turn back to Dax. "Helping us could be more than a little excitement."

Dax nods his chin toward the car. "Gomez filled us in. This was a volunteer run. Everyone was in, so I ended up forcing a few to stay behind to protect the clubhouse. You should have heard the grumbles." He glances toward the car with Beth inside before turning back and giving me a concerned look.

Since the dream about his medical marijuana business became reality, I've worked a lot with Dax. I know his wife, Sofia, well. Their two children are a bundle of energy and spoiled by the big bad motorcycle club members who would die for their leader and his family. Dax's expression is one of concern for a woman and child he doesn't even know.

"She's good," I tell him. "Nervous about the club but good. I didn't go into a lot of detail about you and your men."

"Sofia will welcome her and the baby with open arms. She'll be family in no time."

We look toward the car when Beth opens the door and steps out with the baby. Before I can step in her direction, Dax walks around me and heads to Beth.

"Nice to meet you, I'm Dax," he says and pulls Beth into a loose hug. "Who's this little fellow?"

Beth's large eyes glance in my direction. Dax looks like a skinhead reject, which is kind of what he is. He's wearing a black leather vest minus the club emblem, jeans that have seen better days, chains that hang down for God only knows what purpose, and biker boots that can stomp some serious ass complete the picture. He's grown his hair out and it's tied back to keep it out of his face. His closely cropped beard gives him a sinister appearance. My lips quirk because it's a great disguise. The man is pure baby daddy now. "Um, this is Carson," Beth replies when I give her no help.

"My wife, Sofia, just informed me that I'll be a daddy again in about seven months. We have twins, who are a handful. I don't think adding another will make much difference in the noise level when they get going, and this little guy will fit right in. Why don't you let me hold Carson while you take a trip to the ladies' room? I can change him too if you need me to."

Dax's badassery flies right out the window. He has no shame and I'm not surprised at all that they have another on the way. Of course he has an entire club to act as aunts, uncles, and grandparents. The Desert Crows give outlaw motorcycle gangs a bad rap. They've pulled themselves out of the shit and gone legit. Beth doesn't stand a chance.

Dax reaches for Carson without waiting for Beth's answer. "Here, little guy, come to Uncle Dax." He glances toward the other men. "Say hi, guys. This rascal will be part of the family over the next few weeks."

The men step forward, say hello to Beth, and take turns admiring the baby. Beth gives me a *what the fuck* look and all I can do is shrug. There was absolutely no way to explain this to her. I've been to the clubhouse and seen half a dozen deadly, grown-ass men on the floor setting up a massive train set for the twins. Sofia slapped one of them upside the head for using bad language while the twins took turns sitting on laps, knocking over plastic buildings, and basically causing havoc. Those not involved laughed and called out directions. It was a madhouse.

They still have a few loose cannons among the members but I would easily trust these guys with my life. Hell, I'm trusting them with Beth's and Carson's lives.

"He's been changed but needs to burp. I'll be back in a moment and thank you." She walks into the women's bathroom. Dax puts Carson up to his shoulder and begins patting his back like a pro.

I check out the landscape for something to do. We've crossed into Arizona on I-40, but it's not much different than the New Mexico side of the desert. High desert, though still hella hot.

"Look at those eyes. Kid'll be a looker when he's older. Drive the ladies wild," Curly says. Carson has his eyes open and is staring around at the men huddled around him.

Beth comes out, stretches, and yawns when she's a few feet away. "How much farther?"

She looks tired even after sleeping in the car. Her face is flushed too. "Three hours give or take. You feeling okay?"

She glances at the baby, who seems content in Dax's arms. "I'm good. I don't know if Carson will sleep, though."

"There's no rush now that we're away from my brother's house. We can take it as slow as you need. How are you feeling?"

For some unknown reason, she blushes. "I'm fine," she says quickly. "I've been sleeping entirely too much. It actually feels good to be outside even if it's hot."

"It will be hotter the closer we get to the clubhouse. At least the nights will be decent, unlike Phoenix."

She lowers her voice. "I don't know what to make of Dax and his gang."

I try not to laugh but a chuckle breaks through. I can't imagine what most people make of the Desert Crows. Their outlaw image hasn't really changed. They might run a legitimate business now but they're still a rough group who will do whatever it takes to protect the club. "Give Dax a chance and make up your mind once you know him better."

"Do you think we'll be there long?"

"It could take a few weeks to get everything in place. How long we stay will also depend on Angelo and his father. If they get close, we split. I'll arrange a few safety nets so we have somewhere to fall back on if the shit hits the fan."

Beth walks over and takes Carson from Dax. We hit the road and head for Desert Crows territory.

Chapter Twenty-Four

Beth

I somehow get lucky and Carson sleeps the rest of the way. I'm able to doze for about an hour. Rack pulls into a fast food drive-thru the first time I complain I'm hungry. Having him take care of me has become a habit I need to break. *He* is a habit I need to break.

I eat the fries and burger but go light on the soda because I'm hoping not to stop for another bathroom break. Living this past week without pregnancy bladder has been great and the soreness from giving birth is gone too. Shelby purchased me some jeans a size larger than I wore before becoming pregnant and I managed to slip them on before leaving today. Unfortunately, they're still tight and it's made for an uncomfortable drive.

The scenery changes when we head through the mountains. This isn't what I expected in Arizona. The tall pine trees and milder weather are welcome. It's not green in the way Montana is but the beauty is undeniable. Another hour goes by and we descend from the higher elevation. Rack cranks up the car's air conditioner and the pine trees disappear. I'm enthralled when I see my first saguaro cactus. It's the state tree if I remember correctly. Tall and majestic, they stand out on the hills for as far as the eye can see. They also make me miss my home—the small apartment Nick and I shared before he left for Afghanistan. I'll never return to Montana and chances are good that when I leave Arizona, I'll never return here either. I look at Carson, so sweet and innocent in his car seat. Will this be our life? Always running? I need to stop thinking about it and focus on the positive.   The baby and I are safe for now. A motorcycle gang is on our side. And, Rack is still in the picture. God has my life changed.

Twenty minutes later, we pull off the main highway and hit a dirt road. After a mile and a few turns we pass beneath a large iron sign designating that we've entered Desert Crows territory.

This must be the clubhouse. The building looks new. It has two stories with lots of upper windows and even a balcony. Not the biker gang clubhouse I thought I was heading to.

"These are our new digs," Curly says with pride. "Quite the upgrade from the old shack that almost fell down on our heads."

"The improvement's remarkable. I haven't been here since the remodel started," Rack says.

"You're being a sarcastic ass," Curly says as he laughs. "We tore that old piece of shit down and started over. It's even got a gym. We live the life of luxury now. Dax and his family live upstairs. The main clubhouse is still on the ground floor. Sofia designed the clubhouse kitchen to make cooking for all of us easier. That room alone makes it worth the price. The woman needs to write a cookbook when she's finished popping out kids."

About eight men and women come outside to greet us. Rack brings the car to a stop and the men line their motorcycles up in a perfect row. This is a different world. Several women lock lips with some of the bikers as a welcome home.

A high-pitched squeal from the front door draws my attention. Two naked toddlers run outside followed by a young woman. She's smiling even when she gives a stern command to the toddlers. "Get back here you little heathens," the woman yells. They beeline for Dax and he swoops down and picks them both up. The woman shakes her head. She may be a little older than me but not by much. She's wearing a colorful blue and pink top, a green bandana wrapped around her head, and short shorts. Black, clunky, ankle boots complete her outfit.

What surprises me most is her Mexican heritage. With a naked child under each arm, Dax walks over and plants a huge kiss on her lips. There goes my image of what a skinhead motorcycle gang consists of.

Curly steps out of the car and grabs the little girl from Dax. He leaves his door open and I can hear her squeal when he tosses her into the air. "You little hellion, where are your clothes?" he asks the little girl, who is now yelling, "Do gagain, do gagain, Curry." It's the cutest things I've ever seen and heard. I have no doubt the child is a handful but gosh she's precious.

"You ready to enter the madhouse?" Rack asks from the front seat.

"I take it they're not the big bad skinheads I thought they were?"

He smiles. "Don't let the prison tats fool you. The club has mellowed under Dax's leadership. Sofia also rules with an iron pan if Dax doesn't control the men properly." He nods at the baby. "Let's get the introductions over. I promise you'll be comfortable here. And safe."

Sofia releases Dax and comes around the car before I'm out. She takes my arm and helps me stand. Once I'm upright, she immediately pulls me in for a large hug. "I'm Sofia, the wife of that good-looking man who escorted you here. The naked imps are our twins, Masey and Jonathan," she says after releasing me. "I hear you have a baby." She peers into the car and then runs around the other side and throws open the door. She has Carson in her arms within a few seconds and Spanish bursts from her lips as she hugs him close. It reminds me that she's having another baby.

I've been so worried. Even though I trust Rack, I didn't expect this. Rack walks over and places his arm around my shoulder. "Come on, let's get out of the heat and get you comfortable."

Carson starts fussing and Sofia walks over. "I have a room upstairs for you."

"Thank you." I take the baby from her arms. Rack's arm slips from around me and I follow Sofia inside.

"I'll grab your bags from the car," Rack says behind us.

The front room is huge. It has a giant flat-screen TV, two pool tables, comfortable-looking couches and chairs, and a mirrored bar against one entire wall. There are four ceiling fans circulating cool air. A hallway is on the left side of the room, there's a door opening off the bar, and a stairway on the right. Sofia leads me to the stairs.

She points to the other door by the stairs. "That's the main kitchen and there's a smaller one upstairs. Make yourself at home while you're here. We have a separate outside entrance to the second floor too. I usually use these stairs because it's always good to know what's going on in the clubhouse. These guys need their heads knocked together every day or two," she says and then laughs.

We enter a foyer with three doors. Sofia leads me through one that opens to a living room and then down a hallway to a spacious guestroom. It has a bassinet in one corner and rocking chair in another. They're similar to the ones we left behind. I walk to the rocker and sit down so I can feed Carson. He's gone from fussing to all out screaming by the time I get us situated.

"Dax said you need pretty much everything," Sofia says as soon as Carson quiets.

"I do, I'm so sorry."

"No worries. Anything you need just let us know." She touches her stomach. "We kept the twins' things in hopes of another child. We worked really hard on this little guy," she says as she winks. Her hand rests on a completely flat belly, but I remember those early days.

I smile back. The relief I feel is overwhelming. For the first time since discovering I was pregnant, my tears don't overflow. I hope I'm finally beating the hormones. I peer down and Carson is staring at me. I smile at him and touch his soft little nose. I'm exhausted, but I know he won't be sleeping for a few hours.

"Can I get you anything right now? Water, soda, tea?" Sofia asks.

My mouth is dry from lack of fluids and I know it's not good when nursing. "Could I have water, please?"

"Coming up." She leaves and I look around with interest. Latin culture fills the room. The bedspread has small squares of bright turquoise, orange, and yellow. The walls have beautiful artwork with striking colors. There's an old washbowl on the dresser and a soft brown area rug on the wooden floor.

Sofia walks back in with bottled water. She opens the cap and hands it to me. I down half before smiling gratefully. "Thank you."

She sits on the end of the bed. "I hope you don't mind but Dr. Santos is on his way to examine you and the baby. Dax said you had a home delivery and haven't been checked by a physician."

More relief floods through me and a huge weight lifts from my shoulders. "Thank you. I haven't said anything to Rack. Carson's doing great but I've still been worried. He's my first child and I would feel so much better if a doctor checks on him."

Sofia smiles in understanding. "You'll love Dr. Santos. He's a pediatrician but he'll take care of you too and make sure you're okay."

"Thank you." What more can I say? This is not turning out like I thought it would. Sofia has made me feel comfortable and safe and that makes me think of Shelby. I can't become attached to Sofia. The pain of leaving friends is too hard. Somehow I need to guard my heart and think about the future. I must keep Carson safe and remove him from the dangerous world Rack is involved in. All these thoughts are more than I can handle right now. I need a day to adjust to our new surroundings.

Sofia gives my arm a squeeze. "You're safe here. The clubhouse can withstand an army invasion and the men will never allow danger to enter these walls. This Gimonde guy and his men will never get to you here."

Her words assure two things: Everyone here knows who they're up against and I'm as safe as I can be for now.

Another weight slides off my chest.

Chapter Twenty-Five

Rack

She's in good condition and so is the baby considering neither has been examined since the child's birth," Carlo, also known as Dr. Santos, says scathingly. Santos is Moon's friend. "Beth needs more fluids, which I spoke to her about. If you are still here in two weeks, I'll get a new weight to make sure the baby is progressing normally. Beth told me your brother and his girlfriend helped deliver the baby via Google. I'm not usually one for practicing medicine found on the Internet but even I'll admit they did a good job." His stern voice lowers and his expression intensifies if that's even possible. "I also told Beth no vaginal sex for four to six weeks after childbirth. I want to be sure you understand the consequences of possible infection if she isn't healed properly."

We're in the room Dax set up for me. It's downstairs and little more than a closet. He talks straight and I've always respected him. How do I explain that Beth and I don't have that type of relationship? I can't. "I hear you, Doc," is all I say.

"Now you. Get the shirt off and let me examine your last catastrophe," Carlo grumbles.

I shrug out of my shirt. "Satisfied?" I growl when he runs a finger over the long nearly, healed wound.

"If your ass had stayed in bed like I said, you wouldn't have the nasty scar this is going to leave. The damn wound has opened numerous times and the skin is growing over the stitches. I may need to cut a few from beneath the skin."

Ten minutes later he slaps some butterfly bandages over a few bleeding areas and mutters in Spanish. He leaves and I head to the bar, grab a beer, and sit back on a high barstool. Maybe the buzz will make the doctor's orders about Beth easier to bear. If I knew I would be touching her in three to five weeks, the empty hole in my chest wouldn't be as prevalent. I won't, though. Beth and Carson need to be safe and the life I lead won't do that. One beer, keep a clear head, and don't think about Beth and sex.

Right.

I look around at the rough, bearded, tatted out members of Dax's club. Taking notice of their shaggy appearance easily takes my mind off sex, and a rumble of laughter escapes me. A heavy hand on my shoulder makes me smile full out.

"Want to share the joke, my friend?" Dax asks.

I tip the beer to my lips and shake my head. "No, I'll keep this one to myself. Tell me how life is working for you." I've spent a lot of time with Dax discussing business. He has a good head on his shoulders.

He takes the stool beside me with his own beer in hand. "Business is growing." He smiles at his pun. "We picked up a new strain of sativa from a clinic in Colorado. It's good stuff and we're having success with cloning. On the family front, the kids keep me on my toes, and the wife keeps me in line and my dick active." He takes a drink. "You?"

Like I want to talk about active dicks. Dax hasn't got a clue. "I don't like Moon sticking his nose in this business with Gimonde or that he asked for your help." Yeah, Dax doesn't care for this sentiment. Too damn bad. I keep talking and disregard his clenched jaw. "Doesn't mean I'm not grateful. Gimonde has a long reach and unlimited resources. I don't want my shit putting your family in danger."

Dax waves his beer around the room. "Take a good long look at where you and your woman are. My men are not afraid. This is our territory. Moon feels the same. If this Gimonde dude wants to bring a war here to the desert, he's welcome to. I doubt him and his pansy-ass men can take the heat."

Dax could be right in more ways than one. It's damn hot here and the desert adds another layer of badass to its inhabitants. I saw it in Afghanistan. Acclimating to the weather wasn't an overnight experience. It hardened you, though. The heat either ate you alive or you conquered hell and flipped it the finger. This doesn't mean Gimonde won't hit in the winter. I keep this to myself. "Thank you for coming for us. I should set the record straight, though. Beth isn't my woman. She'll be safely away from Arizona in the next week or so and I'll be taking a long road trip into Mexico."

Dax takes a healthy swallow from his beer before responding. "You keep telling yourself that. I'm not blind. Those sad puppy dog eyes followed her when she went into house with Sofia. Then you kept looking at the door and had to fight not to run inside and check on her." Dax puts his beer on the bar and places his hand back on my shoulder. "Claiming a woman and then resisting the claim is an impossible combination."

"You're an asshole," I say before downing the remainder of my beer too.

Dax laughs long and loud. "Yep. You're putting yourself into the perpetually hard dick club, my friend. At least I get relief on a regular basis. You know you can go knock on the door at the back trailer and one of the ladies will give you a ride if those blue balls get too bad."

"I need another beer," I say and ignore his offer. The last thing I want is some nameless woman riding my cock.

"Sofia's cooking, so I'm heading upstairs for daddy duty. You wanna go up with me?"

The Dax I knew two years ago and this fatherly Dax are two entirely different people. I think about heading upstairs with him but decide against it. The last thing I want is a reminder of what I'll never have. "No, I'll let you have some private daddy time. I'll talk one of your guys into a game of pool. I'm still trying to win a bike off one of these suckers." I knew a few of Dax's men were listening to our conversation and I'm unsurprised when the smack talk begins.

"You wish, Rack-Man," shouts Vampire, Dax's sergeant at arms. "Last time we played, you paid for my new saddle bags. The prospects give me more game than you do."

Dax walks away laughing and heads upstairs. Vampire sets up the pool table and I head over to get my ass kicked because I never lay all my cards on the table until I need to. This will keep my mind off Beth and Carson. First thing tomorrow I'm contacting Gomez to find out where the new identification cards are.

I'm on my third beer and second game when Sofia walks downstairs. Beth follows with Carson in her arms. She has dark circles under her eyes and I'm fully aware she needs an undisturbed night's sleep even though she slept in the car. She gives me a weary smile and follows Sofia into the kitchen. She never complains and I'm ashamed that I can't chance holding the baby and give her a break.

Vampire gives a low whistle. "She's one hot mamma."

It takes a few seconds for me to understand he's talking about Beth. To say my hackles go up is an understatement. Doesn't matter that I have no right to be jealous. She had a baby a week ago and the small bulge at her belly makes her sexier in my opinion. From Vampire's words it's his opinion too. I bend low over the table to take my shot and glance up before my stick connects with the ball. "Look at her again and I'll cram this stick up your ass." I'm not smiling.

Vampire lifts his chin. "Duly noted."

Dax puts up with no bullshit when it comes to the club women, even the ones who live here and make their living by sleeping with the members. That's Sofia's influence more than anyone's. I tuck my head and make the next three shots, sinking the eight ball last. "I believe we're even. Care for best two out of three?"

Vampire rubs his chin. "You're on, but I have the strangest feeling you've been holding back on your game." He racks the balls and manages only two shots before I clear the table. I place my stick on the wall. "I'll give you a chance to win back the bill before I leave. If you don't have anything to bet with, put up your bike. It's a sweet ride."

"You fuckin' prick." Vampire's smiling when he says it.

"As a kid, I avoided dishes by kicking my brothers' asses on our table," I say with a grin on my way to the kitchen because I can't stay away from Beth.

I walk through the swinging door to the sound of women's laughter. Sofia is holding Carson and Beth stands over a cutting board chopping onions. Tears stream down her smiling face. The kitchen is night and day from the barely working old appliances, peeling linoleum on the floors, and cracked countertops from before. Now Spanish tile decorates the floor. There are chrome appliances, including two refrigerators and two stoves. Add in marble countertops and it's hard to remember what the old place looked like. When Dax decided to give Sofia the kitchen of her dreams, he meant it.

Sofia turns Carson around so he's looking at me. His chubby cheeks are red and he's drooling. In only a week, he's changed. My palms grow sweaty and I mentally force myself to look away. Checking in on Beth flies right out of my head and the need to escape fills me. I meet Sofia's eyes. "What time are you planning dinner? I'm taking a ride with Vampire."

She looks between me and Beth and then settles her gaze on Beth, ignoring my question. "Vampire is one of Dax's officers. All the guys go by names they received when they gained full membership into the club. Dax is Dagger. I don't know most of their real names." She juggles the baby like a pro, which I guess she is. His dimpled cheeks and plump arms and legs shouldn't affect me this way. Hell, the last thing I am is daddy material.

Without an answer to my bogus question, I escape to the main room. Vampire is starting a game of pool with one of the other guys. "I need to check security around the property and could use a guide," I tell him.

"Sure." He puts down the pool stick and signals Coke, another of the members, to follow us outside.

The hot air hits as soon as I'm past the door. Summer's in full swing and in a few more weeks humidity and monsoons will replace the dry heat. How people live in places like Montana is beyond me.

"You good?" Vampire asks.

How the fuck do I answer honestly? I don't. "I trust the club, but for my own peace of mind I need to be sure Beth and her son are secure." I do my best to smile. "Humor me."

"Understood. I'll walk you through what we have here at the house and then we can take a ride and I'll show you sentry locations. We can also drive by the repair shop if you need to kill a little more time."

Vampire totally calls me on my bullshit and I let it go. I'm escaping Beth and Carson and looking for any excuse to do it. We both know it. We walk around the compound, which has cameras covering every square foot of property close to the house. I ask a few questions and we head to the bikes. I take Dax's old one. I've ridden it before. Once the hot wind hits my face, I completely understand the appeal of flying free. Dax always told me it takes the pressure off his shoulders and gives him a sense of peace.

It does. It also makes me think about my blood family—my brothers and parents. Staying with Lincoln this past week was difficult, but it also filled a place in my heart. I honestly never thought to see him again and I'm incredibly grateful to have had the chance. With my lifestyle, death waits around every corner.

Vampire points out the location of Dax's men on sentry duty. I pay only half attention while my mind stays on the family I do my best never to think about. My mother's face flashes before my eyes. The devastation in her expression when I told her I was leaving will haunt me forever. I made Andrew's death harder on all of them by turning my back. I'll be the first to admit I wasn't in my right mind. Andrew's death followed by Nick's death took me over the top. Vengeance was all that saved me. I was incredibly selfish and now it's too late.

Beth would easily fit in with my parents and brothers. They would accept her with open arms. Carson would steal their hearts in seconds. My choices mean I can't give that to Beth or to my family. I made my proverbial bed and will pay the price for the rest of my life. A volley of bullets or a knife buried in my chest will be the best I can hope for. I'll die with blood on my hands and I'll die alone.

Chapter Twenty-Six

Beth

"So you wanna talk about it?" Sofia asks after Rack escapes the kitchen like it's on fire.

I shrug and wipe an onion tear away with my shoulder. Even though he left as quickly as he walked in, he turned the heat up in the room by ten degrees. Is it only me who's affected by him like this? A week postpartum and I have trouble concentrating on anything but the contoured outline of his chest beneath his T-shirt and the loose cut of his jeans that hang so sexy from his hips. Damn, I've seen him wearing those jeans too many times to count and I still want to slip my hands inside and cup his ass cheeks. Hormones, I tell myself for the hundredth time before turning my wandering thoughts back to Sofia. "Nothing to talk about. He feels he owes my brother a debt and for the sake of my little guy," I say and nod at Carson. "I'm thankful he came through. I'll never be able to repay him for what he's done."

A stubborn expression replaces the gentle look Sofia had for me a moment before. "If you let that man go, your white ass is dumber than most."

I bark out a laugh. "You don't pull punches do you?"

"No time. Life's short. Me and my man had a lot to work through before we settled in as a couple. It made us stronger. If you love Rack, you'll find a way to keep him." She jiggles Carson on her hip. "This little guy needs a father."

I don't know how else to get the point across that Rack and I won't work. What I say comes out sounding horrible. "He's a criminal. I'm running from one and the last thing I need to do is raise my child with another." I wipe another tear away and this one has nothing to do with the onions. I shouldn't have said that, but this is not the life I want for Carson.

Sofia looks skyward before settling her sharp gaze back on me. "The men here...the ones keeping you safe are who you're referring to as criminals. It's okay, I don't take offense, and neither would they. No one's perfect. The only difference between them and white collar criminals is money. If these guys had money to avoid prison, most would have gotten off and never served a day." She lifts Carson a little higher and kisses the back of his head. "These men live by different rules. We're family and they'll protect me and my children with their lives. I'd rather have them at my back than some holier than thou prick with a credit card and a fancy car. It's a tough, dangerous world no matter which side you choose. My badass family makes it less so. You don't want to hear this but it won't matter where you go once you leave here. You'll look over your shoulder for the rest of your life. The only thing that can keep you safe is a scarier man than the one who fathered this little guy. I guarantee you Rack is that man."

I calmly turn away, walk to the sink, and wash my hands. I plan to spin around and give back as good as Sofia is giving me. I want to tell her criminals are criminals. That everyone has a choice. Instead, I lift my hands and cover my eyes as tears overflow. "I'm sorry," I say after turning. "I fucked up and Carson will pay for it his entire life."

"Buck up, sister." She grins. "Stop feeling sorry for yourself and judging your man. He's a good person and no one on earth will ever love you and this child like he can *or* keep you as safe. I know this because my man's the same way. If you loved this Angelo guy, it wouldn't matter who or what he was. Love is like that. You need to decide if you love Rack enough to overlook his past and make a life together."

I wipe my eyes, relieved that I'm not going into a tailspin breakdown. I gaze at Carson. I want him safe and like Sofia said, I doubt I'll ever feel safe again. She's also right about looking over my shoulder. I don't know about her other observation. Would I have overlooked certain things if I actually loved Angelo? If he felt the same about me and I hadn't tried to escape him, I wouldn't know the truly horrible man he is. How do I know Rack isn't as bad? Sofia makes it sound so easy, but it isn't.

I take the few steps between us and take Carson from her arms. "I'll think about what you've said. Are you still willing to teach me to make your enchiladas?" I pray she'll allow my change in subject. The last thing I want to do is insult her and her family again.

She walks over to the window and removes a string of dried red chilies. "It's all in the sauce, chica. I roast and dry my own chilies and the guys can't get enough."

Red, one of the ladies I met earlier, walks into the kitchen. "Hand that little guy over to nanny granny. I'll sit in here while the two of you cook." She winks at me. "You don't ever want to taste something I had hands in preparing."

We all laugh and the mood in the room lightens.

During the next hour, we chat and prepare enough food to feed an army. Carson is ready for his dinner by the time we put several large platters of enchiladas into the ovens. Red reluctantly hands him over and I go upstairs to my temporary room to feed him and then put him down in the bassinet for a nap. I lie down on the bed, close my eyes, and try to erase Rack's expression when he looked at Carson in the kitchen. Even I noticed the longing in his eyes. I think I understand why he hasn't held my son. Rack is afraid of loving him. The thought breaks my heart.

* * * *

"Hey, sleepyhead," Rack whispers and nudges my shoulder.

I open my eyes to his beautiful face. His body is heated from the sun and his scent is filled with sweat and musky man. Without thinking, I lift my hand and run my fingers across the three crosses tattooed on his neck. "Why?" I ask quietly, aware Carson is still asleep.

Rack's fingers close over mine and he brings my hand to his lips. Whereas earlier I see his longing for Carson, right now I see the same for me. "Two thieves and Jesus." He kisses my hand again. "One thief repents and goes to heaven. The other denies and is damned to hell. When I chose my path, I knew I would never see Andrew again in this life or the next."

My heart breaks. I wasn't raised with religion but it doesn't matter. This man believes he is beyond redemption. "Are you truly a bad person, Rutherford?" He moves my hand so it covers my heart with his on top. The beat is fast beneath my palm.

"I'm your worst nightmare, Beth. I've done things that would make Angelo look like a saint."

I lift my arm, circle behind his neck, and pull him close. He could resist, but he doesn't. I kiss him with all the sorrow I feel. I would cleanse his soul and take away all the pain if I could.

I relish his taste and the feel of his lips against mine. It's my way of soothing his beast and thanking him for rescuing me and saving Carson. His strength is undeniable and so are his demons. His hands settle beside my head, caging me in. It's only the two of us in the small piece of this world. The tender kiss lasts about a minute before Rack takes over. His mouth goes from pliant to demanding. His tongue circles inside my mouth and our world turns to lips, and tongues, and teeth. Passion explodes inside the kiss. My fingers tangle in his hair. We inhale each other's ragged breaths and absorb the kiss into our very pores. This is more than even making love. His lips are sweltering hot and a force of nature. It's been a week since I gave birth and my body doesn't care. I'm on fire. He's only touching my mouth and I'm out of breath, reduced to pants and whimpers. The sexiest growl leaves his throat. I feel the kiss to my very soul.

The moment doesn't last. Carson gives a short cry followed by a longer one. Rack pulls back. Our eyes remain locked. I inhale sharply when Rack runs a finger across my wet lips. "This will only hurt us both," he says over Carson's louder cries of distress.

"I don't care." I'm angry and sad and so in love it hurts.

His eyes search mine. "You should care, Beth. I'm not the man you need."

He walks away, leaving me cold and alone with a screaming Carson. I'm beginning to think that as tough as Rack appears, he runs away from his feelings. Those for his brothers, parents, me, and especially Carson. The pain he carries runs deep. Somehow I need to shatter the wall he wraps around himself and discover the man everyone tells me he is.

Two lives depend on it.

Chapter Twenty-Seven

Rack

I toss my cell onto the single bed and clench my teeth against cussing.

"Fuck it," I whisper under my breath.

Gomez just put me off again. Their so-called connection for identification dried up and they're going another route, which is taking longer. The next step I've planned for Beth and Carson is solid and will keep them safe. I can't carry out the plan without those IDs.

I spoke to Lincoln before making the call to Gomez. There's been no sign of trouble at Linc's end, which seems strange. I'm relieved but nothing adds up. Dax came for us because Gimonde was closing in on my brother's location or so Gomez said. So why wasn't my brother paid a visit? The entire situation makes me nervous because I have no control.

It's been two fucking weeks since Dax took us in. Three since I asked for the paperwork. I can't handle being in the same room with Beth. Seeing her. Wanting her. Needing her like I need to breathe. She's always been gorgeous. Motherhood only adds to her beauty because it shines so brightly from the inside out and attracts me like a moth to a flame.

I've done everything in my power to avoid the house when Carson is awake. I still hear the little noises he makes and hear Beth cooing to him in her soft, silly baby voice. She's one thing and Carson entirely another. I want to claim him as my son. The same way my heart has claimed Beth. It's easier to stay away. I ignore when he cries by heading in the opposite direction.

I'm an asshole.

It's easier to spend my days baking in the sun and running from my feelings than facing them. I've been helping Vampire tear down a few bikes and replace parts at the Crow's motorcycle repair shop right off the highway. A few days ago, he assigned me a bike that needs a lot of work for my next project. I've never been much of a grease monkey, but helping Vampire is better than seeing Beth. Scraping my knuckles trying to get a stubborn oil filter off is better than thinking how damn sexy she is. Her body is round and lush and looks so damn soft my cock is hard for an hour each time I see her. Showers, soap, and my hand are my new best friends. I can't imagine what Dax's water bill will look like when it comes in.

Meals are hell. After seeing Beth and Carson at the table it takes a few beers to unwind enough to sleep. And now, Sofia has decided we're having a fucking party tonight. The club members are getting together and there's no way I can get out of it. My patience is thin, my cock hard, and my mood trashed. I haven't been out of control this bad since Andrew and Nick died.

The music is blasting in the main room and the walls actually thump to the heavy rock beat. Drunk bikers should improve the situation. Not. I pull a T-shirt over my head, tie my shit kickers, and head out. I know there are club members working the perimeter. I'll hang for a few and then replace someone.

I turn the corner of the hallway and enter the main room filled with a bunch of rowdy bikers. They're already wound up and by the looks of it, drunk or heading there with a vengeance.

"Hey, Rack, get over here and have a shot," Vampire shouts. He's standing at the bar with a few of his brothers. One of them moves slightly and I see Beth behind the bar. She twists off a bottle cap and slides the beer to one of the guys.

Holy mother fucking shit. She's wearing some kind of halter top and her breasts are nearly exploding. Thank God I can't see what she has on below the top or I think my dick would detonate right now. Her breasts filled out more after Carson's birth but this is ridiculous. I would give anything to slide my dick between them and get off.

My fantasy comes to an end when one of the guys places a hand over Beth's. I take a step forward. Beth quickly slides her hand away and turns her back. My eyes shift to the guy who touched her. The guy I may need to kill. He's a big motherfucker and has only been with the Desert Crows for a few months. He came from another club in Cali. It doesn't help that I haven't liked him since Dax introduced us. It was something in his eyes—calculating and cold. I've seen it before and it's always ended badly. My hands tighten into fists at my sides. My attention turns to Vampire, who's staring at me. He's wearing a damn smirk because he knows I'm close to losing my shit. During the hours we've worked on bikes, he throws a verbal jab whenever he can about giving my dick relief.

That's the thing with bikers. They fight, they shake it off, and they're still friends when the dust settles. But if I kill the guy who just touched Beth, I doubt the club will kiss me and make up after his blood drains out on the floor.

"You don't want to tangle with Gar," Dax says from behind me.

My eyes scrape across the bar and focus on Beth again. She smiles and laughs at something one of the guys says. "Burning off steam and bloodying my knuckles seems like a good time right now." I don't mention murder, which is what I'm actually contemplating.

"I have no doubt the evening will end exactly how you want it to. But no one will ruin my woman's party in the first two hours," he says with a deadly look that speaks volumes. "I assigned Vampire to watch over Beth for the evening. He won't let anyone cross the line."

I've kept half an eye on Beth but now give Dax my full attention. The burn of his words turns my anger up ten notches. "You knew I'd be here. Why the fuck would you assign another man to watch my woman?" I grind my teeth to keep myself from exploding. The corners of Dax's lips tip to the slightest degree. If he smiles right now, he'll be the first person I deck.

"Interesting," he says lightly. "You've been missing in action for two weeks. Your. Woman," he cocks an eyebrow, "is barely holding it together. She takes care of her baby around the clock and rarely allows anyone's help. From my perspective it's hard to judge whether you're a blind fool or just an idiot." Dax steps closer so his face is inches from mine. "Plenty of guys here are sick of your shitty attitude. They'll be happy to take off a little steam with you as a punching bag. But you will give my woman two hours before blood spills or I'll kick your ass myself."

I'm sucking air into my lungs and having little success holding back the red hot rage.

"No," Sofia growls from a few feet away. "This is my party and the two of you will not ruin it."

Dax backs off, but I don't take my eyes away from his.

Sofia gives me a small shove. "Don't be looking at my man that way. I'll just shoot your ass." Her hand goes to her hip and sure enough, she has a handgun holstered in the belt at her waist.

The clouds clear from my head and I slide my eyes from Dax to Sofia. "Did you give her the damn shirt she's spilling out of?"

Sofia has the audacity to laugh. "You'll also take the fight you'll be having in two hours outside or you'll be replacing what you break." She loops her arm around her husband's waist and all but drags him away from me. Dax gives me a hard gaze before reluctantly walking off. I'm aware I've pissed off the wrong person, and a large part of me just doesn't give two shits.

I take up position across the room so I have a clear line of sight to Beth. If my crossed arms, clenched jaw, and stalker-like gaze don't keep the guys away from her, I'll happily do it with my fists. In two hours. Fuck.

One of the club women brings me a beer. "I'm Dina. You want company?" she asks after sitting the beer down on the table.

Her mistake is blocking my vision of Beth. "No, get the fuck away."

Her hands go to her hips. "How about I crash that bottle over your fat head."

I look up and give her the famous Street stare I learned from my father. "How about you try."

"Dick," she huffs and walks off.

God, now I'm threatening women. It's a new low. I drag my hand across my face. What in the fuck is wrong with me? Thank God she left the beer. I drain it hoping it'll help calm my ass.

The minutes tick by. Beth stays behind the bar. Red's not here, so I'm guessing she has Carson and the twins. Sofia gives me death eyes every fifteen minutes or so, which I ignore. Beth hasn't looked at me once and does everything in her power to avoid gazing anywhere in my direction. She also doesn't chat too long with any one guy, so I slowly start to unwind. I'm not lucky enough to have another beer delivered to my table, so I decide to approach the bar.

I ignore when the noise level in the room drops as I approach. Vampire tips his beer at me and gives the guy on the stool beside him a direct look. The guy leaves quickly. Vampire kicks out the stool another few inches and I take it.

Beth's pouring a tequila shot and the bottle starts shaking. She doesn't look up. I take the bottle from her and finish pouring the shot. She finally glances up. Keeping my eyes on hers, I down the shot.

Bad idea, I say silently. I shouldn't drink more than another beer. And I really don't give a fuck and pour another. This close, her breasts are much more visible than they were across the room. Through the white top I can see the outline of her nipples and all I want to do is kill every motherfucker who's had an eyeful.

Fuck.

Chapter Twenty-Eight

Beth

The clothes I'm wearing were Sofia's idea. She's tired of me sulking and she thinks I need to push Rack on his ass. The fact that my breasts are ready to erupt with the need to feed my son only makes the display I'm putting on worse. I don't look down to see if my nipples are leaking. That would only put a cap on a non-perfect night. To say I've always dressed conservatively is an understatement. I'm far from a prude at least where other women are concerned but for myself, I prefer large sweaters and jeans. Not that you can wear sweaters in the desert in the summer. I have good legs, but living in Montana means there's limited time to display them. Even when I could, I would go for longer shorts and not the ones I'm currently wearing that barely cover my post-baby ass cheeks.

I'm an idiot. It's killed me not to look at Rack over the past hour. There's no doubt he's been looking at me. I feel the burn of his gaze from across the room. Now he's directly in front of me and when I look up, I'm captured by a heat too hot to touch.

He's avoided me for two weeks and now every unsaid word is in his dark eyes. I can't do this. I have absolutely no backbone. "I need to feed Carson." I turn and charge from behind the bar and head through the kitchen to the back door.

I feel him behind me. His hand around my arm makes me turn and it doesn't matter that I'm running, I'm also ready to fight. "No," I say with venom. I disregard the beautiful lines of his face, his lips that make me yearn, his bulging arms that promise safety, his thick neck that I want to sink my teeth into. I shake off the butterflies that fill my stomach just from looking at him. "I'm heading to feed

Carson and you need to do whatever it is you do now and stay away from me."

His eyes blaze. He lets me go. I back up and turn. I feel him watching from the back door when I go inside Red's trailer. Carson is fussing and the ache in my breasts increases.

"He's been hanging in there until just a few minutes ago," Red says when she turns. She's walking with Carson against her shoulder. The twins are passed out on the couch. I've grown close to them these past two weeks. Masey is the exact replica of her mother in image and temperament. I saw Sofia's temper in full bloom when one of the club members swore in front of Masey and Masey immediately repeated it. The man is lucky he walked away with only a bruised jaw. The funny part was the calm before the storm. Sofia took Masey's hand and said very sweetly before escorting her out of the room, "Loki, stay right there, I'll be back in a moment."

Loki was on a ladder replacing a lightbulb in the ceiling of the kitchen. A few minutes later Sofia walked back in as Loki was coming off the ladder. She cold-cocked him and he went to his ass with his legs splayed in front of him and a stunned expression on his face as he rubbed his jaw.

"I've made the rules very clear. I keep the twins out of the front room as much as possible and if they overhear your language it's on me. The kitchen and upstairs are off limits for your filthy mouth. Find some place to eat until next week or I'll put a vice grip around your balls and pop them." Her voice was low and precise, leaving no room for argument.

"Sorry, it won't happen again," he said before standing, folding the ladder, and carrying it out of the kitchen.

Sofia turned to me after he was gone. "It will take me weeks to break that little heathen of saying that word."

I smiled. Sofia smiled. And we both busted out laughing. Sure enough "ass wipe" became Masey's new favorite word. Then there's Jonathan. Where his sister is a little pistol, he's a mamma's boy. He enjoys being around his father and the men but he's always finding his mommy for cuddle time. He loves Carson and even sings lullabies to him when he's fussing.

"Hold babwe," he says whenever he wants to hold Carson. It's the cutest thing and I prop him on the couch with Carson in his arms.

I envy Sofia and her family. Their life has shown me what it means to be happy and loved. It's also changed my opinion on the members of the club and the lives they lead. The respect they give Sofia, the teasing, and their willingness do whatever she asks is undeniable proof that hard men can be gentle too. She takes care of them, feeds them, listens to them complain about their problems, and kicks their asses when they need it.

Then there's Dax. Sofia told me the story about his first wife's death and his prison sentence. Dax and his men might be outlaws but their hearts are good and their sense of loyalty unwavering.

I take Carson from Red's arms and carefully sit beside Masey and Jonathan so I don't wake them.

"Don't worry, they're passed out for the night. I'll move them to the spare room after you return to the party. There's a playpen set up in there and you can put Carson down in it so you can let loose."

Red has been incredibly nice to me. She understood from the start that I don't want Carson out of my sight and she never pushes. Sofia insisted I allow Red to babysit so I can knock some sense into Rack. Too bad I failed miserably.

I smile at Red. "I'm not going back. If you want to go and join Curly at the party, I'll watch the kids. I can fall asleep here on your couch if you'll wake me when you come back."

Red's mouth twitches and she shakes her head. "Every person in this club knows that you and that man should be together. Sofia put this party on for one reason and I'll be damned if I crash her plans."

"You don't understand," I say wearily.

"I understand perfectly." She pushes a wisp of red hair out of her face. "Men let you down and put you down. I've been there, bought the T-shirt, and mopped up their blood with it when I kicked them to the curb. There's no shame as long as you learn from your mistakes. I have no doubt you'll protect that little guy with your life. Your man is your life too and you need to protect him the same way. That means plucking up the courage and taking the first step."

She makes it sound so simple. She's right, though. I was never like this before Kevin and Angelo. My brother would hate the half-woman I've become. "I can't have sex yet," I blurt out before thinking. Heat rises up my neck.

Red's loud laugh startles Carson, but the twins don't move. I switch Carson to my other breast. "I haven't had to give the sex talk in...well never," she says and laughs again. "You got a set of lips on you and there isn't a man alive who wouldn't want them wrapped around his dick." She rolls her eyes. "Okay, maybe Curly only wants my lips and Dagger only wants Sofia's but damn girl, a man will follow you anywhere for a blow job."

Even though I'm embarrassed, I go for broke. "He already turned down a blow job. He got me off and when I offered to return the favor, he said no."

This doesn't shake Red at all. "You get down on those knees of yours and bat those long lashes and he won't stop you. Lick your lips, unzip his pants, and give one stroke with your tongue. He'll be a goner."

I can't believe it's come to this and I'm taking advice on forcing Rack to accept a blow job. Red walks down the hallway and returns with a tube of lipstick. She pops the top off and shows me. "This will do the trick."

It's deep cherry red.

Chapter Twenty-Nine

Rack

I lean against the doorjamb and wait for Beth to leave Red and Curly's trailer. The minutes tick by while I mentally slam myself for being such an ass. Beth will be living a very different life shortly and making her own decisions. I won't be around to make sure a man doesn't touch her or say something inappropriate. She'll find another man. One who will be a father to Carson.

Anger and hopelessness twist inside me. Two cartel members directly responsible for my brother's death are still breathing. I didn't expect it to take this long. I have pictures of them but not names. Killing these last two men has gone far beyond vengeance. I've taken risks and should be dead. On my last trip into Mexico I came so close to getting their names. Gomez and I have put the pressure on rival cartels and it will pay off, eventually. It must.

I carry their pictures in my wallet on the opposite side where I've kept Beth's. I remove them and with the kitchen light shining over my shoulder, I study the two men. Their eyes are what separate them from the people in my world. They would kill their mothers for a step up in their criminal world. They decapitated my brother. I've never found a video but his imagined screams ring in my head. This nightmare haunts my sleep and keeps me on this path. No one's family should suffer like mine has.

I'm well aware Afghanistan changed me. Nothing of the young man who went to war with red, white, and blue dreams of heroism still exists. War does that to you. I remember coming back from two weeks in the desert and finally making it safely behind the walls surrounding the U.S.-built Gardez Hospital. United States diplomats and high-ranking officers have all the luxuries of home while enlisted men, even Special Forces, had tents and dirt floors. We were hot, filthy, and completely exhausted. We hadn't slept in days. For safety reasons, we had to leave our vehicles outside the walls in a covered garage and enter through the gate on foot. Our tents were set up on the east end of the grounds, about half a mile from where we came in. A Humvee driver pulled over and offered the six of us a lift. The vehicles usually transported "important" personnel. We were thankful for the ride and climbed into the vehicle. Before we could pull away, a diplomat flagged the driver. His wife was with him. We squeezed together to make room, practically sitting on each other's laps.

"I can't handle the smell, honey," Mrs. Diplomat whined to her husband. The man told us to get out and walk. I'll never forget how it felt. Hell, they had a fucking spa at their disposal. We'd lost two of our men keeping their asses safe.

Then there was the oil train. The American-built Gardez Hospital has no gas pipeline coming in to keep the electricity running. The oil supply train, which my unit protected many times, is their only source of oil. Car bombs, IEDs, and snipers make the trip long and dangerous. We all knew as soon as the U.S. pulled out, the billions spent on the hospital would be wasted because the Afghan people had no way to keep the electricity running.

Money. Everything has a price tag and that's all they cared about. American lives mean little. I don't care if it's Republicans or Democrats in control of the U.S. government—money fucking rules. The lesson came home even harder when Moon rescued me in Mexico minutes before I got my ass shot. Moon had money and power. He also had a sense of decency. I rarely saw it among the Afghan power brokers, and the drug cartels lack even minor decency.

Add my three tours in Afghanistan, my brother's death followed by Nick's, and all that's left is a black hole that not even Beth can close. I touch the three crosses on my neck. I'm the man who says no to salvation.

I place the two well-worn pictures in my wallet and shove it into my back pocket. I need to focus on the goal. To do that I need the paperwork Gomez promised and I need to send Beth away.

My attention turns to the squeak of the trailer door opening. I stay where I am. I haven't kept Beth up to speed on the plans and she needs to know. I don't care how angry she is. She'll stop and listen to what I have to say. I place my hand out and she shoves me hard against the doorjamb. I laugh at her display of aggression. The laugh dies when she seals her lips to mine. It's everything our last kiss was…and more. Beth's a tiger and she sinks her claws through my shirt into my skin.

Her knee lifts and presses against my hardening cock, causing me to groan into her mouth. I start to pull her closer but she releases me and backs into the kitchen. "I have another hour behind the bar. It won't matter if you run and hide. I'll find you. Whatever shit's been going through your head for the past two weeks is over. If not, leave and don't look back. Dax and the club will protect me."

Before I can answer, she saunters away in shorts that barely cover her ass. Me and my stone-hard cock follow. I take up residence at the table I vacated earlier. I forgo alcohol. Nothing will happen when her bar shift is over, but to keep that reality in check, I need a clear head. Even if I decided sex with Beth was in our best interests, Dr. Santos's words fill my head. "Four to six weeks," he told me. We still have seven days until the four week mark.

"Hell," I mutter. No alcohol. No Beth. No making this entire situation worse than it is.

Vampire nods at me from across the room and points to the hallway to the left. I take this to mean he needs to piss. I nod, keep my eyes on Beth, and think about the kiss she gave me. Movement from the corner of my eye makes me glance away from the bar. Gar, the club member from earlier, is making his way back to Beth.

I sit up straighter.

I can't hear what he says, but Beth's expression changes instantly. I'm out of the chair and five feet closer when she tosses a drink in his face. I have no idea if I'm clear of the two-hour mark, but I no longer give a fuck. I grab Gar by the arms and fling him away from the bar. His entire focus turns to me. He lifts his massive arm and roars. I block the fist he throws at my head and drive upward with a fist to his gut.

The fight's on.

Chapter Thirty

Beth

Does Gar know I had a baby three weeks ago and the pussy he says he smells is a bloody pad? The asshole. There's a glass of soda on the bar one minute and the next it's covering his face and chest.

"Bitch," is all he gets out before Rack throws him aside. Rack's expression is deadly and I'm no longer pissed at Gar. I'm petrified for Rack. Gar has at least fifty pounds in weight and six inches in height on him. Gar doesn't carry the defined muscle Rack has but that doesn't mean Rack stands a chance.

Gar throws a punch to Rack's head and I scream. Rack blocks it and hits Gar in the stomach. "Climb up on the bar so we have the good seats," Sofia says from the kitchen doorway.

She's wearing a huge smile and appears completely unconcerned. "You've got to stop this. He'll kill him."

"After what Gar just said to you, Rack has my blessings."

I had no idea she heard. She's also out of her mind. "Not Gar, Rack," I reply testily. "Gar will seriously hurt him."

"You, sweet Beth, need to have more faith in your man. Like I said, climb up and we'll watch." Sofia moves out of the doorway, steps up on a shelf, and hoists herself onto the bar. She puts her hand out and helps me up. I'm settled just in time to see Gar pick Rack up and slam him on a table. The legs break beneath the weight.

A cheer goes up from the men, and I swear I hate every one of them.

"They don't know what that prick said to you either. No way will the men let that pass. Gar just talked his way out of the club and

Rack will make sure he leaves with a few broken bones." She laughs as Rack jumps up and charges.

The impact makes Gar stumble back a step. Rack drives his fist up under Gar's chin and Gar grunts in pain. Rack steps back, turns, and connects a solid kick to Gar's ribs. Gar leans forward and Rack strikes again with his fist.

"I was a semi-pro street fighter and I'm tellin' you, your man's got moves."

I'm almost able to breathe again thinking the worst is over when Gar manages to grab Rack around the midsection, lift him off his feet, and squeeze. Rack's face is bloody and turning purple. He's throwing ineffective body punches because he's in too close. I'm about ready to grab a beer bottle and crash it over Gar's head, when Rack slams both palms against the larger man's ears and head butts him in the nose. Rack breaks the hold, steps back, and swipes Gar's feet out from under him.

"Fight's over, but we'll let Rack have his fun for a moment," Sofia says as she laughs.

Rack dives on Gar and places one punch after another straight into his face. A minute later, Gar's arms fall lifeless to his sides and still Rack attacks. Curly finally grabs Rack around the middle and lifts him off. The fight still isn't out of Rack. His hands go back behind him and he grabs Curly around the neck.

"Enough," Dax yells. "Drop him, Curly."

Rack swiftly turns and looks sharply between Curly and Dax before his eyes cut to me.

"This is where you show your man some love," Sofia whispers.

I slide off the bar and run to Rack. His arm loops around my shoulder and he pulls me in close. "This piece of shit said something disrespectful to Beth and deserved an ass stomping," Rack says through heavy breaths.

"What did he say to you, Beth?" Dax demands.

Crap, heat rises in my face. I'm incredibly relieved when Sofia steps up to Dax and whispers in his ear. The thinning of Dax's lips says it all. He turns to his men. "Throw some water on this piece of shit and escort him to his bike minus his cut. I made the rules clear when he came here and he doesn't deserve to wear our colors."

The men do exactly what Dax says. Not one of them steps forward and defends Gar. Rack pulls me a little tighter into his side and turns us in the direction of the hallway that leads to his room. He opens the door and steers me inside. "I need to wash that asshole's blood off my hands. I'll be back in a moment and then you'll tell me exactly what he said." It's an order and for some reason I take objection. Is the old Beth finally rearing her head? It's about time.

I nod because if I speak it won't be some simpering woman reply and he does need to wash off that asshole's blood. I glance around. The room is small and bare. Rack's travel bags are on the floor. I look down at my shirt and my breasts practically spill out. I adjust them as best as I can and pull up the waist of the shorts I'm wearing so my muffin baby-top is partially covered. A noise makes me glance up. Rack is standing in the doorway watching.

"Don't do that, you're beautiful." One eye is puffy and changing color. His lip is split. He's my hero. Has always been my hero. The anger I felt moments before disappears. His eyes travel my body with appreciation. Enough appreciation that I actually *feel* beautiful.

"Thank you," I whisper.

He steps into the room and slams the door behind him. The sudden noise makes me jump. His eyes are intense and he's not smiling. In two long strides he's on me. I have no idea what he intends until his right hand hooks behind my neck and he pulls me close.

Then…he kisses me.

His tongue slides across my lips, tasting them before plunging inside. He groans into my mouth when I moan. His other hand slides around to my ass and he pulls me tight against his erection.

The heat of the kiss burns the oxygen in the room and I can no longer breathe. Rack gently bites my lower lip and runs his tongue along the inside. He thrusts his tongue back in seeking more, giving everything. He swirls his tongue to a beat lost somewhere inside us. The kiss is sexy and urgent. Playful and intense. Overwhelming and irresistible. Sex with this man would be the same.

I don't notice his hands move until one cups my jaw and the other slides inside the material of my shirt. My breasts are so incredibly sensitive and somehow he knows. His rough fingers are gentle as they rub across my nipples. They weep a small amount of milk and I try to pull away in mortification. This doesn't stop Rack.

He smears the liquid across my nipples and over the skin of my breasts without missing a beat. The kiss softens and gives back everything he just took.

My head spins. My inner thighs clench. The ache is almost unbearable. For the first time in weeks, Carson isn't at the forefront of my world. Rack is. His mouth tears from mine and he slides my shirt up and over my head.

"Rack," I breathe his name. This needs to stop. I can't fulfill the promise my body is giving him. Then I remember Red's words and realize I can. When he leans in for another kiss, I drop to my knees and lift my arms to the button at his waist.

"Beth, it's okay," he groans.

I look into his deep green desire filled eyes. "This is what I can do for you. Let me," I whisper huskily. The button of his jeans slides through the hole and I pull the zipper down inch by inch. It's like unwrapping a present on Christmas morning. He's commando and his erection pops free. He's amazing. Long, solid, and masculine. I tug the jeans a few inches down his ass and then bring up my hand and circle my fingers around his girth. I cup his balls with my other hand. My tongue flicks out and I taste the tip of him— the salty maleness that holds his musky scent too. His fingers tangle in my hair. I lick along the underside of his cock, starting at the base and feeling every smooth inch on my tongue.

He makes a noise deep in his chest as I slide my mouth over him. He's so large and my jaw widens to accommodate him. He hits the back of my throat and I ease off. I want this to be good for him but I've had little practice.

I never enjoyed oral with Kevin because it seemed perfunctory. He went down on me but never long enough to get me off. I went down on him and he came within seconds. That was it. I was left unsatisfied. Or we had sex without oral and it was over far too soon too. Kevin didn't know or didn't care that he always left me wanting more. Then there was Angelo. He told me when I offered that only whores suck dick. In my weakness over Kevin's betrayal I felt ashamed and yes, like a whore.

With Rack, I'm taking my femininity back. I will satisfy him and in doing so have the return of my power. Not because I can't have intercourse, but because I want to please him in the most intimate way. He's holding my hair but not forcing my movements or telling me what he wants. That throws me for a second because I do want him to enjoy this.

His fingers tighten in my hair when I suck just the tip of his cock and run my tongue around the width. He's answering my unasked question without saying a word. I feel him—his need, what turns him on, what pleases him. I listen to the silent communication that I'm not even sure he's aware of. His breathing grows louder and his hips find a rhythm that I follow with my tongue and lips.

"Christ, Beth, God fuck," he growls.

His balls tighten within my palm and his hips press harder. He loosens his fingers and with a final thrust, his cum pours down my throat in strong spurts. I swallow, and lick, and accept the joy I feel along with the power.

I'm not letting Rack get away. He's mine even if he doesn't know it.

Chapter Thirty-One

Rack

The picture of Beth on her knees with her breasts bared will stay imprinted on my brain forever. After the final waves of orgasm pass, I step back and tear off my shirt. The pants are trickier because I'm still wearing my boots. I put my hand out and Beth takes it. I walk her to the bed and lay her back. Sitting beside her I unlace the boots, slip them off, and then remove my jeans.

She looks unsure. "I can't," she whispers.

"You can," I growl. "I haven't finished kissing you. Dr. Santos threatened me with bodily harm if I touched you before you're healed." I gentle my voice. "I don't think kissing is off his list unless you're not interested." I'm well aware of the assholes Beth has been with. I'm also aware she needs to be in complete control of this.

I lean into her and place one hand on the bed at her hip. "I want to touch these, but I don't know if it hurts." I ever so gently run the back of my knuckles across one breast. She sucks in a breath and I freeze.

She smiles. "It feels good but I'm leaky."

My laugh only increases her smile. "I can handle leaky," I tell her tenderly. "I don't want to hurt you, though." I turn my hand and give a gentle squeeze to her nipple. Small beads of milk form. "I find this incredibly sexy."

She glances at her breast, my hand, and then back up to my lips. Her tongue comes out and she licks them. Will she ask? Does my desire to taste her repel her? I don't think so and I very slowly lower my head and lick the tip of her nipple.

It's not what I expect. The milk is sweet but not sweet, which sounds ridiculous. Ambrosia is what I settle on. I move away and watch her expression while I give her nipple another gentle squeeze. Her feet slide up the bed until her shoes plant flat against the bedspread. Her eyes grow cloudy with desire. I taste a second time and her hands move into my hair. "Suck, please," she sighs.

Feasting on a woman's breast is the most primal behavior for man. We learned the art as infants if we were lucky. My mother nursed all her boys and I remember her nursing Andrew. It fascinated me. I am a full-fledged breast man and if more men thought about the origins, they would understand. It's coming home. Being nurtured. Men only think they're the ones who shield and protect. Women bring life and sustain it. They hold all the strength and power.

I slide my lips over Beth's nipple and gently suck.

She moans and one hand goes to the V of her thighs. She pushes upward against her palm. I slide my hand down her abdomen and cover my hand over hers as her pelvis grinds to the tempo of my mouth. I switch breasts and she cries out. God, I don't want to hurt her. Her sweet pants and sighs fill the room. Her scent and taste fill my mouth.

I peer up. Her eyes are closed, the muscles of her neck tight. She's so close. I increase the suction on her breast and add pressure to the back of her hand. She screams her release into the room and I take her mouth at just that moment. My lips wet with ambrosia, wanting her to taste the gift she's given me. She needs to know how incredible she is.

I love this woman with my entire heart. I love her more than life itself. Does anything else really matter? Lost in her, I don't think it does.

For the next hour we kiss, and whisper, and laugh. She relays what Gar said to her and I almost explode with rage. "No," she says when I look at the door ready to hunt him down and kick his ass all over again. "You're not leaving me."

She's right, I'm not. She talks about the cooking lessons Sofia is giving her. I talk about the bike I've rebuilt with Vampire's help. It feels wonderful to bring her back into my life and to become part of hers. We kiss and talk until she finally falls asleep with a smile on her lips.

I watch her sleep knowing the next step I need to take. Loving this woman is not a half measure. I quietly untangle myself from her arms, slip on my jeans, and leave the room without shirt or shoes. The front room has quieted down and a few men play cards. I pass them silently, head through the kitchen, and out the back door. I knock twice on the trailer door and open it. Red, Curly, Dax, and Sofia are at the table with coffee.

Red's eyebrows go up, and Curly waves me inside.

"I came for my son," I say.

"It's about damn time," Red replies.

"Yes it is. I need his bag too. He's sleeping in my room tonight with me and his mother." I look straight at Dax. "Gar knows too much. I can ask Gomez to pick him up."

"It's taken care of," Dax replies. "I never trusted him. The club he came from was wishy-washy about giving us details about him. I was suspicious and we've kept an eye on him since he arrived. I don't think he'd have said what he did to Beth if he weren't drunk. Doesn't matter. He knew about our connection to Moon and he knew we were helping Moon by taking you in. No choice in what had to be done. Kept it on the down low because of your woman."

"Appreciate it." Moon would have ordered a hit too.

This world never bothered me before and I don't know why I'm disturbed now. It's the life I chose when I came into Moon's organization. There are no do-overs.

I follow Red back to the bedroom and see Carson lying in a playpen. Red places his bag over my arm. I lift him and pull his warm little body against my chest. Home. Family. Love. It all swells within me. I can't look at Red because I'm about to lose it. I walk past everyone, keeping my eyes straight ahead. Curly holds the front door open. I manage the kitchen door myself. I walk silently through the main room and softly close the bedroom door. Carson sleeps on.

I'm done.

My back slides down the door until I'm on my ass. The baby's bag slips from my shoulder and I place that hand on his back. My other is beneath his tiny diapered rump.

I remember Andrew just like this. So small, so helpless. Me and my brothers loved him so much. I don't ever remember being jealous that he required all my mother's time. What I do remember are his smiles. His laughter. His learning to ride a bike with his big brothers beside him. His unwillingness to cry in front of us when he crashed and ended up with stitches in his chin.

My chest aches with holding it all inside. I never grieved for him. I allowed revenge to eat my soul. One tear becomes two until they spill down my face in a flood. I cry for my baby brother who will never marry and have a son like Carson. I cry for my mother who experienced the pain of losing her youngest son. And my father, who is a tough son of a bitch but also taught us to be kind. I cry for Nick. He would hate me for allowing his sister to experience what she did. I should have been there and kept an eye on her. Instead, killing was all I thought about. I destroyed my family. And Linc took me in when I asked. Because that's what brothers and family do.

"Rack." Beth gently touches my shoulder. I'm so lost in sorrow I didn't hear her get up.

I can't look at her. I slip one arm from Carson's back and pull Beth in against us. More tears flow. I was too damn angry to do this when I should have. It was easier to show no emotion and run away. Easier to kill and offer justice that I can never fulfill because there will always be someone who deserves death for their crimes.

Her arms close around me and she says nothing while I cry. "I love you," I finally whisper against her hair. "I love this guy and I've been incredibly stupid thinking that not holding him would keep me from caring."

Her fingers dig into my skin and her shoulders shake. She's crying too—this incredible woman who is so fucking strong. She walked through a freezing forest without complaint. She practically gave birth in a car to keep her child safe. She's everything Nick promised and more. I take deep cleansing breaths. My world is whole and for the first time in years...I'm at peace.

I have no idea how long we remain on the floor. When Carson fusses, we move to the bed. Beth's teary gaze holds hope. I kiss her cheek. "If you'll allow it, I want to give Carson my name. My real name even if he can never use it." I wipe the new tears from her face. "You can think about it. This is a big decision and I have a lot to make up for." I prop pillows behind her so she can comfortably feed Carson.

She settles him at her breast and looks at me. "I don't need to think about it. You've been his father since the moment he was born. I would have told him about you as he grew older. He will never know who his biological father is, only you."

A lump forms in my throat. Now that I've released the pent up pain, my emotions are raw. I lie down beside Beth and watch Carson eat. He's beautiful. They're beautiful together. His little hand fists into Beth's breast and he makes small noises that split my heart in two. I love him.

When he needs to burp, I lift him from Beth's arms and pace the room and pat his back. He's restless until he burps. A few minutes and wiggles later, he falls asleep. "It's your turn to sleep," I tell Beth. "I'll wake you when he needs to eat again."

"He should be good until morning," she says and yawns. "Lay down and I'll snuggle with you both. Tomorrow night you're coming to our room so he can sleep in his bassinet."

I need to call Gomez tomorrow and add my name to the needed paperwork. My mind runs through the list of changes I need to make to our plans. No matter the amount of work required, I'll hold Beth tomorrow night and the night after.

Love changes everything.

Chapter Thirty-Two

Beth

If any woman tells you something is sexier than a bare man chest
while he holds a baby against his shoulder, she's never seen Rack
with Carson. His muscled chest and bulging arms draw my attention.
Carson is so tiny and Rack so damn large. He turns away from me
and now his back has my attention. The muscles ripple as he walks.
I'm shameless and wonder if I'm drooling. I check my lips and
smile. Desire coils in my belly. The need to feel him slide inside me
is explosive and frustrating because I've followed the doctor's orders
to the letter.

It's been a week since the party. I've finally managed to
catch up on sleep and I'm growing lazy. When Carson cries, Rack is
the first one there. We're currently in the upstairs living room. Rack
turns around and sees me watching him. He resituates Carson so he's
facing me. Carson kicks his chubby little legs and I receive my first
full gummy smile. "He knows his mama," Rack says when I dish out
baby talk and play peekaboo with a small stuffed bunny. Anything to
keep my mind off Rack's bare chest.

Rack, on the other hand, has full discussions with our son
and never resorts to the singsong baby voice I use. It's actually
comical to hear him talk about the ins and outs of handguns verses
rifles. Except for nursing, Carson is rarely in my arms. Rack might
have been late to the plate but he takes the daddy role seriously now.

"I heard from Gomez about getting all three of us the papers
we need. He's working on it and said he'd have them in the next few
days."

I keep my smile but it isn't easy. I like it here. The club has accepted us and I'm growing to care for everyone. If you asked me a year ago if I would ever live the life of an old lady, I'd have said no. Now I think I could. Sofia rolls her eyes when the officers meet in private and told me Dax shares ninety percent of what they talk about and she doesn't want to know the rest. She trusts Dax that much.

I've met some of the other old ladies and liked them too. The women who live in the trailer next to Red and Curly's sleep with the unattached men. The old ladies don't mind as long as it isn't their men. I'm aware most clubs aren't like this, but I'm not interested in joining those. My heart is with the Desert Crows.

"Say what's on your mind," Rack prompts when I remain silent.

I lean in and kiss Carson before giving Rack a short, sweet kiss on the lips. "Would we be safe if we stayed here?"

I see the answer in his expression. This man would give me the world if possible. All he can do is give honesty. "No, it's too dangerous for Sofia and the twins."

I understand and I'm sorry I even asked. "Okay. I go where you go and I trust you to keep us safe." It really is that simple. I won't put Sofia and the babies in more danger than our presence here already has. "How about I feed this guy and you and I take a nap?"

Rack sleeping next to me each night has been wonderful and painful too. It's been four weeks since Carson's birth and I stopped bleeding a few days ago. I'll be damned if I wait another week or two before jumping his bones. I feel great and I'm not sore at all. I just haven't mentioned this to Rack.

He hands Carson over. "Take a nap. I need to work on a few things. I'll take Carson while you help Sofia with dinner." He kisses my forehead and walks out. Damn, I need to work on my seduction skills. This woman has needs.

* * * *

When I was young, my brother did most of the cooking. When I was finally at college and on my own, I survived on fast food. After Kevin and I returned from Haiti and I was too in love to know better, I backed off my college classes and devoted myself to him. He preferred to go out to dinner at places where important people would see him. That took cooking off my agenda.

Here, with Sofia's help, I've discovered I love it. She's a wonderful teacher. It amazes me that she cooks in such large quantities and happily feeds whoever comes to the clubhouse in the evening.

"It gives me a break from the twins and gives their father a good dose of toddler terror," she tells me as we shred a mountain of roast beef. Rack is upstairs with Dax. It's become our nightly routine. The men take the children and I follow Sofia to the kitchen.

She's right about toddler terror. Masey decided she didn't want to eat her lunch earlier and wanted a cookie instead. When Sofia said, "No, you need to eat five bites and then you can have a cookie," Masey's entire plate ended up on the floor and her blood curdling scream woke up Carson. Sofia picked the little girl up out of the highchair, cleaned her fingers and face, and then marched her to her bedroom. My heart broke for Masey, who began crying, "Daddy, I want my daddy."

Jonathan started crying too and we had three tearful children on our hands. How Sofia does it with twins is beyond me. The break from all the children is welcome while we cook dinner, and having Rack in the equation helping with Carson makes it sweeter.

"I need to seduce Rack," I say out of nowhere. "I mean..." Sofia has a knowing smile on her face. "We've um, done other stuff but the baby, and um, doctor's orders."

Sofia shakes her head. "Believe me, I understand. You need some alone time with your man. I'll watch Carson. Ask Rack to take you for a ride on the bike he's been working on. I'll move the bassinet out of your room while you're gone. When you get him back here, steer him into your room and jump his bones." Her smile grows conspiratorial. "Seduction is highly overrated."

We both laugh.

* * * *

It took a bit of work to get Rack to take me out on the bike because he worries Angelo could have men watching us. Dax actually comes to the rescue and explains that if any strangers were hanging around Peach City, the town where the clubhouse is located, he'd know. I add in that I'm going stir crazy and need to escape if only for an hour or so. Rack gives in and the first part of the plan is in the bag.

I rode a motorbike in Haiti. It in no way compares to the power of the Harley that rumbles with a loud purr as Rack navigates the winding highway. My hands lock tightly around his waist and my chest presses firmly against his back. Loose strands of my tied-back hair fly around my face as the warm wind hits us.

Rack's hair has grown out even more, but it's still a long way from being in his eyes. I think it's sexier now, and tonight I'll enjoy holding onto it.

Freedom is the only word that comes to mind while we ride. "Wherever we end up, we need a motorcycle," I shout into Rack's ear. He nods in agreement. Once he made the decision to take me riding, the anticipation in his eyes excited me. He's like a little boy with a new toy. He takes so much pride in this bike and it warms my heart that something outside his criminal life can give him a sense of accomplishment.

I enjoy being alone with him too. In the hopes that tonight goes as planned, I pumped milk for Carson. I'm glad Rack can't see my blush as I think about how I looked while working the pump. Cow Udders R Us is how I felt. I wouldn't give up nursing Carson for anything but that damn milking machine Sofia loaned me might curtail our outings unless I can get over my awkwardness. I laugh into the wind for the shear sake of life being so wonderful.

We head toward Payson, which is higher in the mountains than Peach City. Rack drives me past one of the medical marijuana clinics the Desert Crows owns and runs as soon as we hit the main highway and he shows me another one in Payson. A few days ago, we had a long talk about the business Dax runs. Rack explained that all the permits are in Sofia's name and that in addition to taking care of the twins and making meals she's a driving force behind the dispensaries. It's a different world to me, but I care about them, and what they're doing is legal.

Rack drives through winding roads that lead to Strawberry and Pine. We left before dinner and Rack is taking me to a steakhouse in Pine. The mountains are beautiful with the scent of pine trees in the wind. The temperature drops ten degrees. We have extra gear in the saddlebags in case it's colder on our return trip.

It's a Thursday night. The restaurant has quite a few cars and motorcycles in the parking lot. The steakhouse sits back off the highway and is part of a cabin resort. The view, lit by the moon and the stars, is beautiful. I try to restrain my windswept hair after Rack assists me off the bike.

"You're beautiful," he says and pulls me in for a soft kiss before we walk inside. I'm wearing a leather vest and long sleeved shirt Red loaned me. I'm also wearing the jeans I barely fit in when we arrived for the first time at the clubhouse. Sofia had one of the guys pick up a pair of black boots for me too. I actually feel like a sexy biker chick.

Rack is in jeans and a vest similar to mine with a white T-shirt beneath it and his black boots. He has a concealed handgun in the waist of his jeans, which makes me feel safer.

Rack takes my hand and we walk inside. I don't question it when he requests a table away from the windows. I know he's nervous about having me away from the clubhouse. We wait at the bar until a table is available. He drinks a beer and I have sparkling water with lime. Rack barely takes his eyes off me while we sit and wait.

"You're making me feel uncomfortable," I whisper with a small smile.

"You look incredible and I could eat you," he says a little louder than he should.

This is a new Rack. Okay, maybe not new but he's at peace. The change is in every line of his face. There's a calmness about him now. He's giving up his entire way of life for me. I feel no anger or bitterness coming from him. He's happy. I'm happy.

"Tell me about Haiti?" he asks, which surprises me.

I've never told Rack I was in Haiti. "My brother must have mentioned it to you."

"Your brother was incredibly proud of his little sister."

So I talk and tell him about my experience and then about college and the degree I wanted before Kevin came into my life.

"You'll be able to go back to school. You can get a degree and do whatever you want," he says after placing a warm hand over mine and squeezing my fingers.

"For a little while, I just want to be a wife and mother." God, I can't believe I said that. Rack has never mentioned marriage.

He strokes my cheek and moves my head in his direction. "Is that a proposal?" His lips tip up in the slightest smile.

"No...um sorry, I shouldn't have said that."

"Why not?"

It's going from bad to worse. "When the time is right, um, I think we'll both know."

He leans in close and whispers in my ear, his hot breath sending shivers through me. "I'd marry you tonight. Our paperwork will show us as married. It's a done deal, so don't be shy about it."

So much love swells in my heart. Rack leans back and I smile. "Is that a proposal?"

Chapter Thirty-Three

Rack

Earlier in the day I passed Sofia on the stairway and she stopped me with a firm look and raised eyebrows. "You're one idiot for passing up the chance to take a nap in the middle of the day with your woman. Just saying," she adds before continuing upstairs.

Yeah, I'm a man with a thick skull and it takes me thirty seconds to figure out what she's talking about. I think back to the conversation about the nap and Beth's flushed cheeks. I realized tonight was the night and my dick grew hard. It took a few minutes of thinking about bike parts to deflate my erection so I could walk through the main room.

A short while later, Beth asked for a ride on the bike and I knew there was something in play. Her blush totally gave it away. Two hours after reluctantly agreeing, I put a plan in motion.

Now we're at the steakhouse bar and a hostess shows us to a table. Beth has no idea that several Desert Crows members followed us in the club van. I don't want her to know. This night needs to be special.

I order a bottle of wine and think back to long conversations with Moon about the perfect wine. My law enforcement family never taught me the details of fine dining. Moon is as refined as they come. His seldom seen smile and intense eyes hold an intelligence that covers everything from wine to art. I'm a beer and jeans guy myself. But tonight is special and I'm glad some of Moon's tutelage wiped off on me.

Our waiter returns and we go through the ceremony of breathing and tasting the wine. I have him pour a glass for both of us. Beth almost covers her glass but stops herself. I smile and order. Beth wants a large juicy steak and I make it two. The waiter leaves and I lift my glass.

"I'll take a sip but I really shouldn't," she says guiltily. She's had no alcohol while nursing Carson.

"A sip only."

She lifts her glass to mine. "Beginnings," I say, and we both take a drink. After our glasses are resting back on the table, I make my pitch. It's not by any means eloquent. "What I said earlier *was* a proposal, Beth. I love you. Will you marry me?"

I hold her gaze and remove the ring from my pocket, holding it out to her with my left hand. It's not in the velvet box. I left that back in my old room at the club. The platinum band has inlaid diamonds, and I hope she likes it. If not, we'll chose something she does like. The ring actually means little to me. It's what it symbolizes that matters. After I gave in to Beth's request for a ride tonight, I left the clubhouse, drove twenty minutes to Payson, and bought the ring from a small local jeweler. I also sent Curly on another errand, which will complete our evening. If she says yes.

I reach across the table with my free hand and wipe the tears from her cheeks. The answer shows clearly in her eyes and the loving expression on her face. I stand up and walk the short distance between us to pull her into my arms. I don't care who's watching. If I don't kiss this woman right here right now I'll go insane. Her lips are so incredibly soft and taste like lime from her earlier water and red wine. The combination drives me wild and my hand slides to her ass so I can pull her fully against me. Breaking the contact is nearly impossible but I have a feeling we're seconds from someone kicking us out of the restaurant. I move back enough to hold the ring out again.

She lifts a shaky hand and I slip it on her finger. People around us clap and Beth's cheeks flush deep red. I kiss her again. It's required, and the people around don't seem to mind. When we separate, another round of applause ensues and then our audience returns to their dinner.

"Yes," Beth whispers before I let her completely go and we return to our chairs.

We do very little talking. Every few minutes she gazes down at the ring on her finger and smiles. In my post-war life I gave up this dream and now I have it back. Beth and Carson are all I want.

Once we finish eating, I pay the bill, leave a larger than necessary tip, and walk Beth outside. I get on the bike and place my hand out.

"I need my jacket," she says.

"No, we have a room. It's a very short drive." I can't see her blush but I know it's there. Curly rented the cabin and delivered the key to me minutes before Beth and I left the club. It's the nicest cabin at the resort with a hot tub and fireplace. I wonder what the staff thought of Curly with his rough demeanor, bald head, and long beard. I drive down a lane that looks out over the canyon and locate our cabin.

I grab the saddlebags after we're off the bike and then open the door. Except for the bathroom, it's one large room. I turn on muted lights and walk over to the fireplace. One switch does the trick and we have flames. I turn and gaze at Beth. Her strange expression is not what I expected. I walk forward and take her cool cheeks between my palms. "I'll always protect you. If you aren't ready for this, just say so. We can curl up in bed and talk." I give her the famous Street brothers' smile. "And kiss. I love kissing you."

She wraps her right arm around my shoulder and gives me the slightest, cutest pout. "I don't mind kissing but I want so much more." Her left hand goes to my erection and she makes it perfectly clear what she wants.

"Are you ready?" I ask against her lips.

"I'm so ready it hurts."

The small space separating us is no more. Beth moves one hand up and releases my neck with the other. She grabs the vest and rips the snaps open. With a chuckle, I do the same to hers. Between laughter, because of our boots and kisses, we manage to get our clothes off. When we're naked and standing in the soft light, I lift her in my arms and carry her to the bed. I don't rest her down gently—I toss her high so I can hear her laugh. The dark world I left behind is no more. Beth is my sunshine and laughter rolled into love. She's everything.

Once her body sinks into the fluffy bed, I ruffle through my clothes and remove three condoms, tossing them beside her. I pounce. There's not a square inch of her that will be left un-kissed. I've feasted on her breasts this past week, so I leave them alone for now and start at her neck. I run my nose across the soft skin that smells so delicious. I nip her throat with my teeth and feel her sigh as much as I hear it. I leave a trail of wet kisses while I explore.

Her hands knead the skin on my shoulders. She digs her nails in because if nothing else I've learned about her sexual appetite, she enjoys marking me. I suck a section of skin at her neck and her nails give an extra bite.

"Please, Rutherford," she breathes heavily against my shoulder. I love when she says my full name. Only my family used it up until now. Beth *is* my family. She and Carson. I kiss down her chest and past her breasts until I'm at her belly. Her body has changed since giving birth. She's lost weight. But this. The softest place on her entire body still has a small pooch that turns me on like nothing else. I circle her bellybutton with my tongue and her tummy quivers with laughter. God, I could slide my cock over her stomach and come.

My lips drift downward. I leave a trail of love bites across her skin. She grabs my hair, digging into my scalp when I slide my fingers over the sensitive flesh of her sex. I haven't touched her here since she was pregnant. She moans and her warmth closes around my finger when I slide it inside. I inhale Beth's sweet earthy scent into my lungs.

"Rack," she sighs. My lips follow my finger and I kiss the folds of skin nibbling just the tiniest bit. God, she drives me wild. My dick is rock hard and so incredibly ready. Too fucking bad. I plan on feasting first. I flick my tongue over her entrance and add another finger. She's so deliciously wet. I slide my gaze up her body. Her eyes are closed and her head tipped back.

"You're missing the beauty," I breathe against her.

Her eyelids flutter and then open and my tongue dances across her again.

"Rack, please."

"Come for me like this and I'll give you anything you ask."

She gives a rough, sexy laugh that turns into a groan when I slide my fingers out and back in. I dance my tongue across the hard nub of her clit and then suck it past my lips. I could spend hours right here, feeling her response and taking her to the edge and back again.

Her ass lifts from the bed. "Oh, God, oh, God," she cries.

I love seeing her like this. Uninhibited, reaching for ecstasy, giving me everything. I slide my finger, silky with her wetness, back to her ass and slip just the tip inside. Her eyes have closed again but they open when my finger moves deeper. I won't take her ass tonight but she's so receptive it won't be long until I possess all of her. She pulses against my fingers, one in her pussy and the other in her ass and clenches my hair tighter as she comes undone.

I give her no time to recover. Hell, I don't think her orgasm has stopped. The condom wrappers are tangled in her hair and I pull out a few strands in my haste to get one on. I rip open the package with my teeth and slide it over my cock. I cover her body with mine so her breasts squeeze against my chest. We melt together—skin to skin, heart to heart. I go to one forearm and separate us enough so she can breathe. I nudge her legs apart and push inside her warmth, one slow inch at a time.

She gasps, a cross between a cry and a moan. "Are you okay?" I groan into her hair while trying to stay as still as possible.

"No, no, no, don't stop. You feel so good, don't stop."

I smile into her hair and feel a rush of love so intense it hurts. With another forward thrust, I'm buried balls deep. Her fingers glide to my ass when I start moving. I drive in and out of this wonderful woman while fighting for control. Each moan, each deep breath, each sigh she makes is so fucking sexy. I hold back until her fingers are drawing blood and she's pushing up against me when I sink down. I unleash everything I have until there's no me or her. We're a combination of fuel and flame set to ignite. My balls grow tight and the pending explosion looms as I increase the speed and drive into her again and again. The bite of her nails and her scream takes me to the Promised Land. With one final thrust my body combusts and I groan against her throat.

This woman is mine. Forever.

Chapter Thirty-Four

Beth

We have six perfect hours. We slept little and filled the time with touch and promises. Around two in the morning my breasts became a painful reminder that I need to feed our son. Rack takes enjoyment in relieving some of the pressure, but it's not enough and we're forced to leave this special place behind.

During the ride back more than my breasts ache. The rumble of the motorcycle between my thighs lets me know how truly fantastic last night was. It's a naughty sensation that makes me smile against Rack's neck. He has a filthy mind and he filled me in on all he plans to do to my body. Just thinking about it makes me wet again.

As we approach the clubhouse, milk leaks from my breasts and I'm thankful for the leather vest. I also ache to hold Carson. We pull up and I can hear Carson's wails from outside. We hurry in and Dax is holding him while Carson screams his heart out. With a look of profound relief, Dax hands him to me. Tears stream down his tiny face and his little lips quiver with distress.

"Mama's got you now, sweet boy," I soothe. He wants none of it and continues screaming.

"Here," Rack puts his arms out. "I'll carry him up."

I fly up the stairs and lie back against the pillows on the bed. As soon as I move aside my shirt and bra, Rack hands him over. My breast is so swollen that positioning my nipple in a screaming baby's mouth isn't easy. Once he latches on, I look up at Rack. The evil man admires my naked breast that's a size bigger than it was when we left the cabin.

He shrugs when he sees me watching him. "Can't help it," he says with a smirk. "That's a whole lot of sexy." Rack makes it seem so natural that he's turned on when I feed Carson. I admit his eyes have a way of turning up the temperature in a room when he looks at me with such lust. The man has a serious kink for breast milk.

He joins me on the bed and rolls to his side so he's facing me. "What are you thinking about?" he asks. Heat rises in my face and he laughs. He runs his fingers across my swollen breast while Carson sucks. "I'm always thinking of these," he continues when I don't answer his original question.

"Of course you are, you wicked man," I say with a laugh.

"I want five of these."

I look down at my breasts in bewilderment. He's crazy.

Now he laughs. "Five babies," he clarifies.

Five breasts aside, the man is still crazy. "You're kidding."

He leans in and kisses Carson's cheek. "I always wanted five." His gaze returns to mine. "It seemed like the perfect number after Andrew was born."

"Can I think about it?" I say because I just had one baby and the thought of four more is not exactly lighting a fire under me right now.

He kisses the top of my breast and up my neck, ending with a sweet kiss on my lips. "I'll take just you and Carson if that's where you want to stop. I only wanted you to know that I'm open to discussing more."

"Four more?"

"If you want six or seven, you might be able to change my mind."

He's teasing me and to see this side of him is the most incredible gift he's given me. "I was thinking an even dozen," I say with a smile. He laughs and I fall in love all over again.

We put Carson back in his bed and get a few hours of sleep. When sunlight shines through the curtains, Rack sits up and runs his finger down my cheek to my throat. "I need to talk to Vampire about a skip in the bike's engine and then I need to get a workout in. If I want to father twelve children, it'll take a lot of endurance and I need to be prepared."

My laughter follows him out of the room. I actually think he would have twelve kids if I agreed. Carson's eyes drifted shut a few minutes after I began feeding him but I need to burp him and feed him on the other side or I'll be forced to use the cow milker. Sofia sticks her head in the room after I've switched sides.

"Did the little guy survive?" she asks with a smile.

"I noticed you were nowhere to be found when he was screaming his head off."

She gives a slight laugh. "Truth. He woke up grumpy and it went from bad to worse. I escaped with the twins and let the baby whisperer handle it."

"Believe me, no one was whispering or they wouldn't be heard over the screams." Now I feel really bad for leaving him.

"It was only DEFCON 1 for about forty minutes. No worries, you and your man needed the break."

I hold up my hand and show off my ring. "Yes, we did."

Sofia actually squeals and plops on the bed beside me to admire it. I've gotten to know her well enough and I didn't think squealing was in her feminine arsenal.

"It's beautiful," she tells me. "When's the wedding?"

Her question is the only thing that can make me sad right now. "No wedding. We'll get our new identification and be married on paper. I don't care though," I lie. "Whatever our name is we'll be Mr. and Mrs."

"Nonsense. Curly Sue is an ordained minister. He did it so he could marry club members so we didn't need to ride to the courthouse in Payson. He'll marry you. We can put this together in a few days. I'll bake a cake and we'll order a dress online and have it overnight expressed. Red can do any adjustments needed."

"What? Wait." She's speaking too fast and I don't think I'm hearing her correctly. "I can't get married in the next few days," I say emphatically.

She rolls her eyes. "Sure you can. It will be official on all but court documents and in a week or so you'll even have the paper."

My heart swells with longing. "I need to speak with Rack."

"Of course you do. That man will give you anything. Now let's discuss the cake. Chocolate, white, or banana with whip cream frosting?"

* * * *

Rack agreed and a small ceremony here at the clubhouse turned into a full-blown wedding with flowers, a reception immediately after the party, and a beautiful floor-length white dress. The plans took two days and the wedding is on day three. When Sofia wants something done quickly she has a passel of biker dudes at her bidding and the job gets done. The woman is a force of nature.

Chapter Thirty-Five

Rack

I need a copy of *Weddings for Dummies*. Dax and I are sitting at the club's bar drinking beer and trying to stay out of the way. Every woman connected with the Desert Crows has flooded the upstairs. That entire section of the house is off limits. When the children get in the way, they're herded down here for the men to handle. The wedding ceremony will take place at two o'clock tomorrow afternoon and the plan is to slide straight into the reception from there. We men are to make ourselves scarce tomorrow until the ceremony and that includes down here.

What the hell did I agree to? It sure as hell wasn't sleeping on the old bed down the hallway. "I may not be up on outlaw motorcycle club rule shit but if everything I've heard is true, you need to take control of your old lady and teach her who's boss," I tell Dax.

The guys, including Dax, burst out laughing. "Yeah, like that's gonna happen. My woman has a mean left hook and I don't want to be on the receiving end. She wrote new rules when she took over."

That earns some grunts and good-natured shoves from the men.

"She cooks, makes sure the place is clean, and is also responsible for the new digs we're currently in," Vampire says. "You remember the old clubhouse that was falling down around our ears? It was a dump." He waves his beer around the room. "I'll take this any day. At least they don't have us cleaning outside."

"That's because outside is spotless," Dax chides.

Curly releases a long sigh. "If I remember correctly, you made us clean it up the day after you took over the club and you still get on our ass if we leave shit out there."

"I make us look respectable even if it's a lie," he grins. "And that outdoor cleaning exercise was the best day of my life."

Several of the guys laugh. Johns, who stays fairly quiet, pipes in. "Sofia almost shot you." He shakes his head. "It might be the day you met her but I doubt she'll remember it as fondly as you do."

Dax bumps his beer with Johns'. "True words."

I know the story. Sofia planned to kill her father, a very bad man, who abused her mother. Dax beat her to it and Sofia wasn't exactly happy about it. Add in that Dax was trying to clean white supremacy scum from the club, Sofia's Latino heritage, and you have a situational fireball that Dax somehow put out.

"I say we switch it up to whiskey shots and plan to ride tomorrow morning to clear our heads. We'll be back in plenty of time for the nuptials," Dax suggests.

Cheers go up and Max, a new prospect, pulls out the first bottle of whiskey. This means a hangover on my wedding day, but hopefully the ride will clear it out. This is my last day as a bachelor and a little extra alcohol is fitting. Not that I'll miss bachelorhood for a second. It's been a long road to settling the demons that have haunted me since my brother's death. With Angelo waiting in the wings for the rest of our lives, my abilities and connections will be what keep Beth and Carson safe.

I take my first shot.

* * * *

My head is fuzzy but I'm no worse for wear when I wake up. I didn't drink as much as some and I swallowed a few aspirin before heading to bed. The women had their own celebration upstairs. I managed one quick kiss on Carson's cheek and a slightly longer one on Beth's lips before the women threatened to strip me nude so I could be their bachelorette boy candy.

That got me out of there fast.

I turn down the offer of an early morning ride from Dax and decide to head into Payson for a haircut. I'm almost ready to walk out the front door, when my cell rings.

"Rack," Gomez says when I answer.

"What's up?" I'm hoping this is the good news I've been waiting for.

"Got the paperwork but need to go over a few things. Can you meet me at the warehouse in an hour?"

I check the time. It's nine thirty in the morning and it will take me about an hour to get to the warehouse. I can have my hair cut in Phoenix and be back here with time to spare. "I can give you an hour today or longer tomorrow." I haven't told Gomez or Moon about the wedding because they don't come to the clubhouse. I've been the go-between this past year between Moon and Dax so we could keep Moon's affiliation with the Desert Crows quiet.

"An hour will work." He disconnects.

The Desert Crows take their security seriously and Dax curtailed the drinking of the men who would stay behind today while the women did their thing. Doesn't matter, I have a strange feeling in my gut. *Like getting married wouldn't put it there*, I tell myself and shrug it off.

The women have moved all the tables out and are in deep cleaning mode when I walk through and head to the bike.

"What are you doing in here?" Red demands.

I raise my hands in classic surrender. "I'm going, I'm going." I still look around for Beth but she's not down here. Red lifts her broom and I increase my stride and clear the front door with her grumbling behind me.

An hour later, I pull up in front of Moon's downtown warehouse. There are two vehicles parked out front. One is part of Moon's fleet, the other unknown. The funny feeling I had earlier increases and lifts the hairs on the back of my neck. I almost turn the bike around and leave. This comes down to trusting Moon and Gomez. I walk to the door and open it.

The first person I see is Moon. His cold expression says a lot. The push of steel to the side of my head clues me in that this isn't a social visit and the people I think of as family betrayed me. Gomez, who is standing next to Moon, steps forward and removes the gun tucked at the back of my waist. I breathe in slowly, ready to disarm the man holding the gun and take my chances.

Gomez knows me too well. "Our men have just picked up your woman and the baby. How this goes down depends on you."

The harsh finality of the words stop my next move and the air leaves my lungs. To betray me is one thing, to endanger Beth and

Carson another. "You bastard," I hiss. I've always known the world I entered to find my brother's killers was deadly. I just never expected the killing blow to come from Gomez or Moon.

Our phone conversation in the past weeks have been stilted. I wasn't happy about the delay in paperwork. I should have known something was up. The old me would have. I let my guard down and now Beth and Carson's future are at risk.

Moon nods to the back of the warehouse. I follow him while Gomez waits for us to pass and tucks in behind me. The room we enter is very familiar. This is Gomez's playground. I have no idea how many men I've seen die here. The chemical smell of disinfectant fills my lungs. The outer walls of the warehouse are steel, but this room has inner padded walls to contain the sounds of torture and death. There are no windows and no way out except the door I just entered. A drain is located in the concrete floor. Evidence washes away easily. Gomez keeps a change of clothes on shelves built next to a utility sink so his suits remain pristine while he works. If you betray Moon or go against his strict rules, this is the last place you will ever see.

The questions running through my head are unthinkable until I see Angelo standing to the left of the door. Gomez pushes hard between my shoulder blades and I stumble. I right myself and turn to Moon. "Do anything you want with me but don't give him Beth."

Moon's dark eyes drill into mine. He's in one of his impeccable dark suits, unaffected by the hot temperature, and, like always, in complete control. He lifts his arms and then drops them back to his side. "My hands are tied, my friend," he says without a single crack in his cold expression.

One plus one equals two. Maddison or Celina, possibly both, are in danger. It's the only way this scenario could happen. It's the one thing that would tie Moon's hands and make him give up Beth and Carson. It leaves me with no leverage.

Two men step from the shadows. I've worked with them for years. Cal moves in close and takes my right arm. I trained him and the move is stupid on his part. I explode before Marcus grabs my other arm. If Angelo gets his hands on Beth and Carson, my life doesn't matter.

I slam my elbow into Cal's head and my knee takes Marcus in the groin. Cal strikes back with a side kick, but I grab his leg, turn, and push him into Marcus. An explosion followed by a sudden jolt of burning pain to my leg takes me down. I blink several times before I make sense of Gomez standing with a gun—his last bullet fired now buried in my leg.

Fuck, it hurts.

"You know, cabrón, I do not like guns," he says mildly. If Moon is cold steel, Gomez is molten lava. Neither man makes excuses for what and who they are. Gomez waves the gun haphazardly at Cal and Marcus. "Do the two of you think you can secure him now or do I need to shoot his other leg?"

They drag me to the chains attached to a wench at the ceiling. Within minutes I'm standing with one leg for support, bleeding profusely from the other with my arms secured over my head. Gomez strides to the shelves and sink, removes his shirt, and slips on black gloves with slow precision. What's coming is my second-worst nightmare. Losing Beth and the baby comes in at number one.

Gomez walks to me with a first aid kit. He slices my pant leg and wraps a bandage firmly around the bullet wound. How horrible it would be for me to bleed to death before the fun begins. Next he cuts off my shirt.

When our eyes meet, I whisper, "They have your women, I understand." His expression changes for a millisecond before returning to the sizzling eyes that relish death. I thought Celina changed him. I was wrong. His first punch hits me in the gut. All the air explodes from my lungs. I still can't breathe when the next one lands.

Gomez kills with his fists. I'm a gun man myself, though when it came to the men who killed my brother, the thought of torture never bothered me. I have no doubt I'm paying for that now. Gomez is methodical in what he does. The pain is just beginning.

Fifteen minutes later, my torso is bloody from my bleeding nose and bruised from the steady pounding of Gomez's fists. One of my ribs cracks and the difference in pain tells me my right lung is most likely punctured. I spit up blood and wheeze. It won't matter, Gomez can easily keep me alive as long as he needs to. He eases up on the strikes to my chest and focuses on my face. Within minutes, my right eye is swollen shut and my nose broken. The pain has gone from a sharp reminder that I'm still alive to continuous agony with no highs or lows. The lights of the room fade in and out through my one good eye.

"Enough," Angelo shouts. "The deal is Beth watches him die. You bring her here so she knows what's in store for anyone who helps her."

Garbled blood and spit spills through my swollen lips when I try to speak.

Moon turns to Angelo. "You want the woman here, make the phone call and keep your end of our deal."

Angelo speaks into his phone. "They have him and he's as good as dead. They're delivering Beth and my son. Send the men and I will notify you when the child is here." He puts the phone away. "It will take approximately fifteen minutes for them to arrive."

"I'll have the woman delivered at the same time," Moon responds. "Gomez will give Street a break so he isn't dead before the woman arrives."

Moon hasn't used my real name in years and his use now pisses me off, which helps clear the cobwebs from my brain. He's bringing Beth here to watch me die and the rage I feel far overshadows the pain.

My attention returns to the man beside me with blood-covered gloves. "You don't really want to be awake for this, cabrón." Gomez slams his fist into my jaw and the lights go out.

* * * *

Beth's screams bring me out of the darkness. She's holding Carson against her chest swaddled in a blanket. All I see is one small sock-encased foot. I've failed her and my son just as I did Nick. I should have sent her away weeks ago and discovered another way to obtain the papers she needs. She and Carson will pay the price for my selfishness. Her screams turn to a low keening when Moon wraps his hand around her upper arm and holds her back.

Angelo storms across the room and tries to grab Carson. Moon releases Beth and places his hand out. "We've met your conditions. You owe us." Cal reaches out, grabs Beth, and brings her to his side.

"That's my son." Angelo moves closer to Moon. "You have no right to keep him from me."

"Get her out of here," I gasp between painful breaths. I have no idea why Gomez knocked me out before inflating my lung with a tube. The pain of having Beth watch me die is far greater than anything Gomez could do. I spit blood from my throat so I can speak louder and direct my words at Angelo. "He's my son, you piece of shit. My son!"

Before Angelo answers, two men are shoved through the door from the outer room. Both have hoods over their faces and their hands bound.

"Take the hoods off," Angelo tells his men who follow close behind.

Two Hispanic males with heavily tattooed faces are revealed. Angelo's men push them to their knees. I know exactly who these men are and nothing makes sense. They beheaded Andrew. I blink blood from my one good eye and wonder if I'm hallucinating.

Angelo steps closer to me. "Kill this piece of shit and the men are yours." His gaze turns to Beth. "You steal my son and think you can hide. There is nowhere on this planet where you could ever be safe. The Gimonde family will always hunt you down and we'll kill anyone who helps you. This is your final lesson. I will kill you myself if you ever run with my son again." He turns to Gomez. "Finish this piece of shit off."

The ringing of Moon's phone is all I hear besides Beth's crying. Moon says something into his phone and I turn my gaze from Beth. Moon nods at Cal and Marcus and then the room explodes in gunfire.

Angelo and his men crumble. At the same time, Gomez moves in front of me and Moon tackles Beth. Gun smoke fills the room and Gomez's hand settles on my shoulder when the gunfire stops.

"She's okay, Rack. We've got it covered. I'll have you down in a moment."

Before he removes the chains, Beth pushes him away and throws her arms around me. Everywhere she touches hurts and I never want her to let go. The baby is no longer in her arms; I see the bundled blanket on the floor. Nothing makes sense.

"The baby?" I whisper into her hair.

"Carson is fine. He's with Sofia. It's a doll, Rack."

The winch slowly lowers me. My legs won't hold me up and Beth sinks to her knees, cradling my head. I have no idea who our enemy is. I want to fight but I have nothing left.

Dr. Santos kneels beside us. I don't know when he arrived. "Mio Dios. Señor Gomez had better stay away from me for the foreseeable future or he'll find himself minus cajones." He unlocks the chains from my wrists and checks my pulse. "IV line first and we'll put pain meds in it."

"No," I say emphatically. "What the hell is going on?" The world has gone crazy and I'm barely holding onto my sanity.

Moon's voice floats into my head. "It's a long story, my friend. Right now you'll do what Carlo says. Once you're stable, I'll explain everything."

I try to rise. Beth and Santos hold me down and I slump against the cold cement. "I'll kill you," I manage to spit at Moon.

A slight chuckle leaves his throat. "I have no doubt."

A needle stabs into my arm and Santos hangs a bag of fluids from the chain above me. Beth's fingers run through my hair. It's the only place on me that doesn't hurt. Moon hands her a wet cloth and she gently wipes my face.

Through the fading light I hear her whisper, "I love you."

I'm too out of it to reply. The world goes dark.

Chapter Thirty-Six

Beth

Shortly after Rack left, Dr. Santos came to the Crows' clubhouse and explained that Moon's organization, along with the Laterza crime family, were making a play against the Gimonde organization. If all went as planned, I would never need to worry about Angelo again.

My wedding day.

The doctor said Moon was holding Rack and trading the three of us—me, the baby, and Rack—for two people Moon wanted. The doctor assured me the trade would never go down and once Laterza took out Gimonde senior, Moon would do the same to Angelo and his men. The doctor was talking about killing. That stopped me for a minute. As long as Angelo and his father were alive, Carson and I would never be safe. That was the cold hard truth.

I said nothing about the wedding to Dr. Santos. He could make what he wanted out of the preparations. I left Carson with Sofia knowing she would protect him and never allow Angelo or his father to get their hands on him. Sofia wanted me to wait for Dax to return, but I refused. Rack trusts Moon and I would do the same. I also trusted the doctor. I dressed a lifelike doll of Masey's in one of Carson's outfits, added baby booties to the plastic feet, and wrapped the doll in a lightweight baby blanket. It wouldn't work if Angelo got a good look but Doctor Santos assured me the disguise only had to hold briefly.

It took an hour to get to the warehouse. When I entered the room and saw Rack's condition, I thought Dr. Santos betrayed us. If

I'd had a gun, I would have killed Moon, Gomez, and the doctor without thinking twice. I held on tightly to the baby doll and couldn't help wondering if I would ever see Carson again. I refused to look at Angelo.

Rack's face was almost unrecognizable and the bloody hands of the man standing beside him told the story. At first, I thought Rack was dead. A man stopped me from running to him. Rack lifted his head and I realized he was alive. I was finally able to breathe again, though the world was now a narrow tunnel.

The man next to me stopped Angelo from getting to me and the baby. My brain finally registered that the man was Moon. I was barely aware of what was happening as more men entered the warehouse. Two with hoods on their heads were forced to their knees.

Angelo threatened me, Moon answered his phone, and all hell broke loose, which finally pulled me out of my zombie-like state. Moon pushed me down and I hit the ground hard. I couldn't care less that bullets were flying; all I wanted was Rack. I pushed Moon's hand aside when the gunshots stopped and he tried to help me rise. I was so damn angry. Ripping off his fingers with my teeth was a very real possibility.

I ignored the bodies of Angelo and his men. Touching Rack and feeling him flinch only raised the level of my rage. I didn't know how to help him, and I swore to myself if he died, I would kill the men responsible. Rack's vengeance at the people who killed his brother made perfect sense for the first time.

I rode in the back of Moon's SUV with Rack's head on my lap. Whatever the doctor gave him knocked him out. His steady breathing was all that proved he was alive. I barely remember the next few hours. I couldn't tell you a single thing about our surroundings. Rack had all my attention.

Dr. Santos worked on him for two hours. He had a chest tube, numerous stitches on his face, and bruises covering his chest and face. Dr. Santos removed the bullet from his leg and told me there would be no lasting damage if Rack followed doctor's orders when he regained consciousness.

I'm forgiving the doctor for taking me to the warehouse because he's almost as angry as I am over Rack's condition. He muttered profanities until Rack stabilized. Then, he looked at me with a sad expression, his eyes dark with concern. "They live violent lives and have chosen their paths. Don't think too harshly on it. Sometimes men must do bad things to balance the evil in this world."

He may have been talking about Moon and Gomez but his words fit Rack perfectly. Now that I've seen Rack's world firsthand the realization hits—there is no place for me and Carson in Rack's life. I also understand the importance of avenging his brother's death. It will eat him alive if he doesn't. Carson and the life I want for him need to be my number one priority. Passion has clouded my brain. I love Rack, but long ago he made the decision to live a life of violence and death.

A few minutes after the doctor leaves, one of the last people I want to see enters the room. Moon's imposing figure only ignites my anger again. I won't deny he's gorgeous. The ruthlessness that lurks inside does nothing to detract from his charisma. He looks at me with such intensity that I'm surprised when he speaks gently. "Carlo said he'll remove the chest tube in two days. Knowing Rack, he'll be up and around the same day. My wife, Maddison, and I would like you and your son to be our guests until Rack is able to leave."

I bite my lip to keep the words I want to say inside and respond as pleasantly as possible. "Thank you, but no. If someone would give me a ride back to the clubhouse, I would appreciate it."

Moon sticks his hands in his pockets and looks at Rack. "He needs you to be part of his life." His gaze once more captures mine. How he knows what I intend is beyond me, but somehow he's figured out that I'm leaving Rack. "I know this is hard, but I'm asking you to give him forty-eight hours before you make a decision that will affect your life and that of your son. I think you owe him that much."

Guilt rolls over me as I'm sure Moon intended. I do owe Rack, but I don't like this man reminding me. This was my wedding day and everything went to hell because of his power play. It would be nice to curl up in a ball and cry. But I'm no longer that woman. I have a son who depends on me. Forty-eight hours will make no difference and dammit, I owe Rack a goodbye.

"Are we safe here?"

I see the tiniest trace of relief in Moon's gaze. "Yes, and when you leave, you will be safe to go where you please. The Gimonde family will never bother you again. You have my word."

He leaves after that and an hour later, I'm holding my son. I've been given the room beside Rack's. Maddison, or Mak as she prefers to be called, and Celina made sure I felt welcome. The women's concern for Rack was genuine. I don't know if either is aware his condition is the fault of their men. I won't be around long enough to be involved in that mess, so I keep my mouth shut on the issue. I have no idea why Moon and Gomez played this game to the extent they did. It makes no sense.

The women leave me alone to nurse Carson. When he's asleep, I place him in the center of the large bed and surround him with pillows so I can check on Rack.

I enter the room and Gomez is speaking to Rack in a low voice. Rack's one good eye follows me when I step closer to the bed, and Gomez stops talking. He turns and without thought, I punch him in the jaw. He takes the hit squarely and waits to see if I'll do it again before raising his hand to his face. He rubs his fingers across the reddened area while appraising me. I refuse to show how much my damned hand hurts. His jaw is rock hard.

Rack's sudden chuckle turns into a cough. He sits up slightly and gasps for air. Pain lines his face as he tries to breathe.

"I'll leave the two of you alone," Gomez says and exits the room.

Rack settles back against the pillows and grins. "Not many people live to see another day after hitting that man."

I can't believe he's making jokes right now. "He deserved it. I hope Celina doesn't mind. She *seems* like a nice person."

His grin widens and he pats the spot beside him. He looks horrible—eye swollen shut, nose swollen, and bruises everywhere. He notices my hesitation and his grin disappears. This isn't the time to tell him my decision. Reluctantly, I sit down, lean in, and kiss his brow. It's not that I don't love him but I know that leaving him will be difficult and I'm trying to protect my heart as much as possible. Even with the damage to his face, my stomach clenches because he's beautiful—bruising, swelling, cuts, and all. I take his hand and lift it to my lips.

"I'm sorry," he says. He looks at my fingers and I know the exact moment he realizes I'm not wearing the ring. I release his hand.

"When Dr. Santos picked me up he said I would most likely be in the same room with Angelo. I didn't want to make things worse than they already were so I left the ring back at the clubhouse."

He holds my gaze and his expression tightens with something besides pain. He's searching my eyes and it's difficult to hide how much I love him or that he won't be part of my life. "Come here," he whispers. I lean into him again. He slowly wraps his arm around me and holds me to his shoulder. "It's okay, Beth." His arm tightens a fraction. "Carson will always be my son. Tell him the good things about me. I'll make sure the two of you are taken care of. The only thing I ask is that you allow me to say goodbye to him."

He's breaking my heart. I should have known he wouldn't fight what was best for me and Carson. The love I feel for this man overwhelms everything else and the thought of leaving him is nearly impossible. We stay like that for a long time. Eventually, I realize he's fallen asleep, and I slip from the room to check on Carson.

He's still sleeping. I crawl on the bed beside him and allow my tears to flow.

Chapter Thirty-Seven

Rack

For two days I'm as weak as a newborn. The first twenty-four hours are a fog. After that, the pain and my inability to do the most basic of tasks made me beyond grumpy. Beth brought Carson in to see me often. The ache in my heart is worse than the ache in my chest cavity where the doctor inserted the tube after removing the one that Gomez put in.

I'm not sure how I feel about what Moon did. It ultimately makes little sense and I've lost my trust in him and his organization. I will never forgive Moon or Gomez for bringing Beth in to see what Gomez did to me. The fury running through my veins stays bottled inside.

For now.

I told Gomez to empty my offshore account and set the money up in Beth's name. I want her and my son cared for. I don't need the money even though I have no idea what I'm going to do with the rest of my life. I will no longer be part of Moon's organization. I will return the money Gomez put in my bank account while Beth and I were on the run.

"I can tell by the look on your face that I'm just in time," Carlo says from the doorway. I can tell he has just come from his office because he's wearing some kind of child friendly T-shirt with black slacks.

"About fucking time," I mutter.

He walks in and places his medical bag beside my hip. "I'm removing the tube and you'll be able to walk around more," he says, ignoring my bad mood. "I know you won't listen but you need to take it easy for the remainder of the week."

"You're right, I won't listen," I reply as he removes the tape from my chest. The tube is attached at the other end to a pump, which rests on the floor. Apparently it's been pumping out air from my lung cavity while the puncture in my lung healed. As far as I know, none of Gomez's victims last this long, so I wasn't familiar with the remedy for a collapsed lung.

"Removing the tube won't be too bad. Unfortunately, the broken ribs will remain sore for a month or longer. Breathe in for me."

I suck in air.

"Let it out."

He pulls and the tube feels like it takes my insides out with it. *Won't be too bad* my ass. He places two stitches in the hole the tube leaves behind and puts another bandage in place. He tries asking a few questions, but all I do is grunt. He pokes and prods for a few more minutes before packing his bag and leaving.

I rise from the bed as soon as he's gone. I struggle to get into a pair of pants because of my ribs. I'm panting and sweating by the time I zip and button them. I walk out of the room and hear Beth's voice coming from next door. She's sitting on the bed playing with Carson. He smiles as she makes weird noises, spirals her finger, and plucks his tiny nose.

This moment.

His smile.

Her voice.

I burn them into my memory.

I must have made a sound, because her head whips around.

"Hi," I say.

I follow her gaze when she looks to the wall beside the door. A rolling suitcase and Carson's diaper bag rest there. This is it. I step forward and she pushes herself off the bed and into my arms.

I won't beg her to stay because I more than understand. She's safe now. This world, even though I'm leaving Moon's organization, stains my soul. I will never shake the things I've done. I hold her while keeping my eyes on Carson. So damn close. I almost had it all.

She's crying softly. I have no reassuring words. My ribs are killing me but I squeeze tighter. "May I have a few minutes alone with Carson?" I whisper into her hair.

She steps back and wipes tears from her face. "Yes, of course."

I reach a finger out and trail it down her cheek. "Thank you for sharing him with me. I will never forget the two of you." My chest is heavy but I've been here before—denying grief, refusing to allow my tears to flow. Beth needs me to be strong.

"Moon called a car for us," she says. She wipes more tears. "How do I ever thank you?"

She's beautiful and so fucking strong. I could ask for nothing more for my son. "You take care of him and you find happiness," I tell her, though it kills me inside.

She nods and walks to the bags. She lifts the diaper bag over her shoulder and rolls the other bag behind her. "I'll come back up and get him in a few minutes." She leaves me alone with Carson. I wanted to ask where she was going but stopped myself. It's better I don't know. My attention turns to the small child kicking his legs on the bed.

He's in a blue onesie, leaving his small legs and feet bare. His baby hair is messy from playing with his mother. I sit on the side of the bed and run my palm over the wispy strands. "You have a big job on your hands for such a tiny thing," I tell him. The lump in my throat makes it hard to say the next words. "I need you to look after your mother. No, not right now, but when you're older. She has a way of finding trouble." I pause for a minute when he smiles at me and kicks his legs again. "I love you, Carson Andrew. You need to grow into a good man like your uncle and your namesake. Our blood runs through your veins because I'm giving you a piece of my soul."

I pick him up and pull him into my shoulder. His baby smell washes over me. I look up and see Beth standing at the door. She's crying, or has never stopped. I'm having a difficult time holding my emotions inside. This needs to be over now or I don't think I can let her and Carson go. I place him in her arms and kiss her cheek. I leave and head straight to my room, closing the door behind me. The window I'm at faces the back of Moon's property. I stare outside glad I won't see Beth and Carson drive away. I have no idea how long I stand there, when there's a knock on the door and Gomez steps inside.

"Are they gone?" I ask him.

He nods. "Moon wants you downstairs if you think you can handle walking that far?"

I almost say that I no longer give a fuck what Moon wants but I stop myself. "I'll make it," I reply.

After putting on a shirt and boots, I take the stairs slowly and follow him. Once we're on the bottom floor, he heads to the back of the house. Another two turns and I realize where we're going. It's a wet room. Moon doesn't like violence at his home but sometimes it can't be avoided. When I walk inside, I know exactly why I'm here. Gomez closes the door behind us. Moon is standing with a gun pointed at two men on their knees. It's the two from the warehouse. The men who killed Andrew.

Strange really because I haven't wasted a single thought on them. Moon lowers the gun to his side and walks to me. "These men are yours." Moon hands me the gun.

I take it and walk forward. I'm in no condition to do all the things I've dreamed of doing to make them suffer. Killing them should be enough. Both men stare me in the eyes. You don't get to their level of cold-blooded killers and beg for your life. When you live like they do, you know if you're lucky it will end quickly with a bullet. I lift the gun.

Beth's face flashes before my eyes.

Carson's smile.

My brother's laugh.

Nick's smirk.

My mother's face when she scolded us boys.

My father's police swagger when he walked.

All the things these two men took from me. I look at the gun in my hand. An extension of my hand. So much blood that no one but my nightmares see.

I lower my arm, turn to Gomez, who's standing closer, and hand him the gun. "No." I look between Moon and Gomez. "I'm no longer that man. I don't care what happens to this scum, but it won't be me who hands down their retribution."

I walk to the door and leave the room without looking back. I'll go to my brother Linc's house and start from there. I walk several feet down the hallway that leads to the stairs. The door to the entertainment room was closed when I walked past it a few minutes ago. It's open now and I glance inside. Beth is standing in front of a large television screen. The screen shows the room I just left, the two men still on their knees, Moon and Gomez standing over them. The screen goes dark and Beth turns. She's holding a sleeping Carson in her arms.

My rage builds. Not at her but at Moon and Gomez for taking a chance that I would have killed those men with her watching.

"You didn't do it," she whispers over my son's head.

"That's no longer who I am."

"I know." So much love shines from her eyes. My anger at the circumstances melts.

In three strides she's in my arms with Carson squeezed between us. I hold her as tightly as I can. A noise behind me makes me lift my head from her shoulder. Gomez stands in the door.

"You were never one of us, cabrón, and it's time for you and your woman to move on. There's a car waiting out front. Thank you for being my friend."

It all makes sense. The deal with Angelo. The two men I left alive in the room. "What if I would have killed them?"

Gomez shakes his head. "You were never a killer. Circumstances forced it on you. Moon never doubted what you would do even if I didn't exactly agree. You proved me wrong. If you ever need us, we'll be there. But somehow, I doubt you will. Your brother was never in danger. We needed you closer to keep you safe and put Moon's game into play."

He turns and leaves before I can say anything. I release Beth so I can lift the diaper bag and suitcase. What broken ribs? I'm on cloud nine and feel no pain. Beth and I walk outside to the waiting car. We drive away.

"Where are we going?" she asks.

"We have unfinished business at the clubhouse, but we need to stop and pick up a marriage license first. Shit," I mutter.

"What?" she asks with concern.

"My ID. I want you taking my real name."

She leans over and grabs the diaper bag, which is in front of the car seat that was inside the car. She takes out her wallet and hands me my license from so many years ago. "Moon gave this to me."

Moon gave us more than that. He gave us life.

Chapter Thirty-Eight

Beth

The wedding took place the next day. We're headed back to the cabin we stayed in almost a week ago. The only thing missing is the motorcycle. Rack didn't want me out of my wedding dress even when I told him I could put it back on in the room once we arrived.

"No way. I'm taking this dress off." He kissed my fingers over the ring that will never be absent again. The wedding took place earlier than our originally scheduled time and it's still daylight.

He picks me up and carries me over the threshold into the shadowed room. "Your ribs," I laugh.

"My ribs will survive, Mrs. Street."

He draws in a sharp breath and I know it hurts. Damn man. He puts me down and wraps his arms around me. My laughter disappears. His lips move over mine and he licks the inside of my mouth. For an unknown amount of time all he does is kiss me. I've never known a man who gets so much enjoyment out of kissing. Of course, I've never known a man like Rack. He's better than my brother's letters ever described.

"I love you," he says when he finally lifts his head. His face is such a mess of cuts and bruises.

"I love you," I reply because I love him with my heart and soul.

"Now the dress," he whispers with a wicked smile. I slowly turn and present the small buttons that run from the neck to the hem. Rack's fingers work their magic starting at the top. His hot breath hits my skin before he kisses every inch of flesh uncovered as the buttons give way. I'm wearing a tight white corset beneath the dress. "What's this?" he whispers again.

"I had to look good in the dress," I whisper.

"No, no, no." He begins untying the laces. "You're perfect. No contraptions or I'll need to look for a plump wife who understands how sexy she is."

I love him so damn much. The corset gives way and I'm able to take a deep breath. He lifts me again and carries me to the bed. He grimaces with pain when he leans over and sets me down.

I try for the meanest expression I can muster considering it's my wedding day. "No more picking me up." He undoes his tie and I go silent. He takes off his suit jacket and slowly unbuttons his shirt. My heart beats double-time when he peels it off. Triple-time when he sits on the bed, removes his shoes and socks, and then stands and takes off his pants and boxers in one downward pull. I still have heels on and I lift a leg.

He takes my calf and kisses the top of my foot. "These stay until I make the fantasy of fucking you in them on a reality." He licks the skin and then gives the slightest of bites. He releases my leg and moves enough to comfortably run his hands up my thighs to the bottom lace of my panties. He runs one finger under the elastic and slides it across my wet sex. I want him so bad it hurts. He swings one leg over me so he's leaning over the tops of my thighs. He kisses his way to my breast, finds my nipple, and sucks until my hips lift from the bed.

"God," I moan.

He laughs and slides my other breast free. I couldn't feed Carson before we left because of the dress and corset. I pumped milk the last two days so we could have a wedding night. This time I was smart enough to pack the milker. I still feel uncomfortable while it's doing its thing.

"You taste divine," Rack whispers.

"You're a kinky bastard," I tell him with another long sigh.

"The kinkiest. I need to keep you pregnant so I can enjoy this for years. Twelve babies, remember?"

"You wicked man," I say and laugh. "You want to keep me the size of a house."

One hand leaves my breast and travels to my tummy. "This needs to stay like this or bigger. A house means a whole lot of lovin'."

He moves up from my breast and kisses my neck. "I love you, Beth Street."

"Say it again." I sigh.

"My wife, Beth Street." He supports himself with his left forearm and slips the fingers of his other hand beneath my panties. "These need to go." He slides them down and I lift my legs. The panties get caught up in one shoe.

"You're evil for making me keep the heels on," I chide.

"Maybe." He nuzzles my neck and then bites. I inhale sharply and forget about the shoes. "Lift your knees, Beth, and wrap those gorgeous legs around me."

With panties still hung up in my shoe, I do as he bids. He positions himself over me and his cock slides home. I press the heels into his ass and wrap my hands around his back, sinking my nails in deep. He glides slowly in and out finding a rhythm that drives us both wild. His lips come down on mine and his tongue dances to the same beat as his cock. I forget about everything but my husband.

He breaks off the kiss. "Hold on." He rolls and takes me with him so I'm sprawled on top. "Ride me, Mrs. Street."

We're still joined. I lift my knees slightly and rest my hands on his chest. He palms my breasts as I set the rhythm. This is so good, so perfect, so wonderful. My pussy tightens and heat builds between our bodies. We are an extension of the other. One body, one soul, and a love so big it heals everything.

I'm close.

"No, not so fast," he groans. "Move up here, I want to taste you." Oh, God, he's going to kill me. "Ride my face, beautiful." He releases my breasts, slides his hands around my waist to my ass, and pulls me off his cock. I grip the headboard as he lifts me higher and I'm kneeling over his face. His tongue swirls and I cry out. He sucks and nips and sucks some more. His tongue slides into me and I have no word for the noises I make. His hands grip my ass and lift me up and down.

The air around us is dried tinder ready to ignite. When it does, I scream. He lifts me again and I fall onto his chest. I'm too undone to think about his ribs. He positions my weak limbs so I'm over him again and his cock fills me. He rolls us back to the other half of the bed and increases his tempo. His heavy groan is followed by my own cries as our world explodes together.

Chapter Thirty-Nine

Rack

A one-night honeymoon wasn't enough. We both missed Carson, though, so we made it work. We're back at the clubhouse and I'm nervous. I stare at my phone for several seconds before I touch my brother's name.

It rings twice before he answers. "Detective Street."

"It's Rutherford."

"Are you okay? Beth, the baby?"

I hear the worry in his voice and hate myself all over again for causing it. "We're good. Do you have a few minutes to talk?"

"Go," he answers.

I tell him what's happened, excluding the warehouse scene.

"Are you responsible for Gimonde and his son's death?" he asks me.

"No," I tell him. "I wasn't aware of what was going down. I'm not unhappy about it, though."

"Yeah, okay. Can't say I was unhappy to hear it either. Where does that leave you?"

"I want to come home."

There's a long minute of silence on the other end. "When?"

"We're leaving here tomorrow."

"Shelby and I will move her things to my side of the duplex and you can have her place. She won't mind. She's mentioned it a few times since I told her the Gimondes were no longer a threat."

"Thank you." My voice cracks and Beth, who's sitting beside me holding Carson, squeezes my arm. I move my hand down and place it in hers. I inhale. "I'm calling Mom now. We'll be going to see her and Dad before we get to your place."

"Thank God. She needs to know she's a grandmother."

My chest hurts and it has nothing to do with my ribs. "I'm so sorry, Linc."

"I love you, Rutherford. I'm glad you're coming home and bringing your family."

The call ends a minute later. Beth leans into me and I circle her hip with my arm. With one hand I punch in the number to my parents' house.

"Hello?" My mom's warm, loving voice fills my ear.

Dear Reader,

Wipe those tears. I loved ending this book with the sound of Rack's Mom's voice. I truly hope you enjoyed this incredible man's happily ever after. I promise Rack will appear in the books about his brothers, Calvin and Woodrow. Street Fight and Street Law are part of my future book releases.

A few details to help you better understand Ignite:

I seriously dug myself into a hole with Beth's pregnancy. These books are hot and steamy and I kicked off this story with a woman who is eight months pregnant. Thank God I remember my pregnancy hormones going wild. I also want to add that I have always thought breastfeeding beautiful. I nursed my three daughters and it was such a special bond. Dads really need to be more involved in it just like Rack. And yes, that's a kinky statement.

My youngest daughter delivered her baby at home with only her three year old for company. Definitely not planned that way but it gave me comfort in Beth's refusing to go to a hospital. I had so much fun with Shelby Googling child birth. I also enjoyed giving you another dose of Daisy. You haven't seen the last of these characters either.

Gardez Hospital is in Afghanistan. A police buddy told me the story of the soldiers returning and then being kicked out of the vehicle by a diplomat's wife. I don't remember the actual name of the hospital he mentioned and used Gardez because it exists. My friend's story made me quite angry and I wanted you to know that it happened in real life. Thankfully I believe in Karma.

Speed Radar is a detective's best friend. Not only does it do its job and slow down traffic at key points but it also logs all license plates that drive past and holds the information for up to six months. You have no idea how many crimes I solved with this little bit of technology. So yes, to all you conspiracy theorists, the government is watching.

Special thanks to Jerri Mooring for naming baby Carson. Honorable mentions go to Wendy Higgs for Gracie and Haleigh Carlton for

Addison. It would have been a toss-up on the two names if Beth's baby were a boy. These three ladies belong to the Fang Readers Group on Facebook where I host the naming contests. If you're interested in joining click the link above.

Moon worked quite a lot behind the scenes of this book. Someday he and Maddison will have another story. He's such a great character but when he's bad, he's very, very bad.

I have another outlaw story to write and I can't decide if I should do one of the Street books first or just kick off with Combust. The decision will leave my hands when the little voices start talking in my head so I'll just wait until that happens. Just a hint… the outlaw made an appearance in this book and also Sizzle. He's as hot as they come.

The next book on my agenda is "Like a Girl" another football story and yes, you'll get some Killian MacGregor. This book is humorous, intense, and so, so hot.
Thank you once again for entering my world and supporting my work. Please take an extra step if you have time and leave a review where you purchased Ignite. Without reviews, my books aren't seen. I will really, really love you if you do.

Peace, love, and hope,
Holly

Author Bio

Holly S. Roberts is a retired homicide and sex crimes detective who loves long walks on the beach and sweet music. Not really... she hikes mountains with her Rottweiler and listens to hard rock with heavy bass and bad words. She's the USA TODAY Best-Selling author of the Completion and Hotter Than Hell series. If a book doesn't have enticing romance, steamy sex, and hot alpha men she doesn't read or write it. She writes paranormal stories as D'Elen McClain so if you enjoyed Crimson Warrior, look her up or visit her website for links to all her books at wickedstorytelling.com.

Also by Holly S. Roberts

Hotter Than Hell Series
HEAT
SIZZLE
BURN
STREET JUSTICE
IGNITE
COMBUST

Completion Sport Series
PLAY
STRIKE
KICK
SLAM
RUCK
LIKE A GIRL
LIKE A GIRL SEASON TWO

Club El Diablo
DAMIAN
ZACK & MONROE
MONROE & ZACK

Made in the USA
Middletown, DE
19 December 2018